A COPPER GRAVE

A MARK HAYES STORY

BRENT TOWNS

ROUGH
EDGES
PRESS

A Copper Grave
Paperback Edition
Copyright © 2025 Brent Towns

Rough Edges Press
An Imprint of Wolfpack Publishing
1707 E. Diana Street
Tampa, FL 33610

roughedgespress.com

Paperback ISBN 978-1-68549-568-8
eBook ISBN 978-1-68549-567-1
LCCN 2025948120

Never the grave gives back what it has won!
—Friedrich Schiller

The grave is but the threshold of eternity.
—Robert Southey

A COPPER GRAVE

PROLOGUE

Thirty Years Ago...

Les Jones eased his horse to a halt and surveyed the table-flat land stretching out before him. It wasn't just a cursory glance, but one of love. This was the driest, harshest, toughest piece of dirt he had ever seen, but he'd managed to eke a living out of it, which made it even more special. Apart from his family and rodeo riding, this wasteland was the biggest passion of his life.

It was, however, in desperate need of rain, two years passing since the last great downpour. But once it came, the transformation would be unbelievable. No one, not anyone, would take it away from him.

Les turned in the saddle as he heard the bleating of sheep off to his right. There was a line of them coming toward him. To the south, the crackle of thunder signaled the passage of a distant storm. The sky was dark, and he could see the heavy curtain of rain sweeping across the land, punctuated by jagged forks of lightning. If only it would come further north to fill his dams.

That's what Les was doing—checking dams. Some

were getting too low, like the feed in the paddocks, which meant he would have to move stock around. Maybe in another week or two, before he went to Queensland for a stint on the rodeo circuit.

Another rumble of thunder, this one a lot closer than the others. Les's horse shifted nervously beneath him. Reaching down, he patted its neck reassuringly, soothing the animal with his voice. "Easy, boy. It's just the big fella shifting some furniture around."

Les looked up and saw the ominous clouds roiling above him. He frowned. The storm couldn't have moved that quickly. He looked back to the south and saw the storm still tracking on its original path. No, there was one forming over him.

"Looks like we're going to get some rain after all, boy," he said in a low voice. "Time to go."

Using just the pressure of his knees, the bay started to walk forward.

Suddenly, a jagged fork of lightning dropped from the gray clouds like the fist of God, striking the only tree for miles. The tree sparked and seemed to explode. The sound of the thunder was deafening, and this time the horse lurched wildly beneath him. It took several minutes and all of Les's skills to bring him back under control.

"Easy now," he murmured.

The first drop of rain landed heavily on his shirt, leaving a circular outline of moisture. It was soon followed by another, and another, until the landscape was covered with the wet gray curtain of the sudden squall.

Les urged his mount on. Being caught out in the open with lightning all around wasn't a place he was eager to be. Another lightning bolt crashed earthward, followed by the deep boom of thunder.

There was a lean-to he'd built for the sheep beside the

next dam. It was scant cover, but shelter was shelter. He'd head there.

For the next ten minutes, Les rode through the unabating storm. If anything, it had intensified. The bolt of lightning had now turned into a sheet, and the sky illuminated constantly with bright flashes.

The horse slopped through hoof-deep water as the hard-baked earth refused to let the water penetrate it. Then, ahead of him, Les saw something. The horse stopped. Les peered into the gloom and saw the movement again. It looked to be another rider. Out here? Who'd be this far afield on his property?

Les removed his Akubra so that he wouldn't have to look through the water cascading off its brim. He narrowed his eyes and caught sight of the rider again. "Bloody hell," he muttered.

Then, replacing his hat, Les urged his horse forward once more, determined to find out who the rider was and what they were doing on his land.

CHAPTER ONE

Present Day...

Day 1, Monday

They were words that later I would come to regret hearing.

"I want you to find the person who murdered my father."

But Mark Hayes knows best, and besides, I needed the work. Upon hearing the statement, I sat up straight, pain coursing through my body. I guess I should tell you why. When the opportunity arose, I was recovering from my latest sojourn to the dark side of the law—investigating the loss of a beloved family pet.

Hearing the animal's name should have been enough to knock back the job. I mean, who calls their bloody dog Monte? Crap always seems to follow me somehow.

The life of a private investigator in the country. Country? I was so far away from civilization that I wasn't sure which side of the Black Stump I was on. Maybe the east side. Just. The burning fires of hell would have been more appropriate.

A lot has happened since I last spoke to you. For starters, Nicole was transferred to Hopetown from Friar's Lake. I think it had something to do with me. However, Nicole doesn't think so. Her pregnancy is progressing well. Helen, the daughter of crime boss Pete Agosti, left our care. That was a government decision. Not ours. And there are a few other things. But we'll get to that.

Hopetown is in western New South Wales—yes, just like Friar's Lake but drier—on a strip of dry river called the Warren. Watercourse is an ambitious description because it was lucky to run once a year, if that. Only when the rains from up north filtered down was it allowed to flow and restore life into the system. But now, it was as dry as a week-old piece of sourdough. The town would be too if it weren't for the copper mine. The lifeblood of Hopetown. No mine, no town.

Before I go on, let me tell you a little about myself. You already know my name and the fact that I'm a private investigator. I'm a little over six feet, mid-thirties, and at one point in my life, I was a cop. Briefly.

Long story.

It took me a day to find the Monte. Not many places in Hopetown where a dog can hide. In a culvert, under a bridge, beneath someone's veranda. Not in the long grass of a vacant block. The lack of water saw to that. This time of year, vacant blocks were nothing more than rocks and dirt.

However, of all the places I'd looked, the garbage dump wasn't one of those I'd considered. But there he was, tossed aside like yesterday's rubbish, on a pile of rotting kitchen scraps escaped from a torn bag. This was following his death during an illegal dogfight run by the local funeral director. Who would have thought? Bodies by day, dogs by night. I was surprised that he wasn't burying the dogs at the same time he was interring the humans. Would have made perfect sense, right? But how many funerals does a hick-town funeral director do in a week? Must have been a slow week. And some criminals just aren't that smart, as you will see.

I said it took me a day to find the dog, which was right. It took me another few days to get to the bottom of the "organized crime" syndicate stealing Precious Pup and Co. from the backyards of the family homes.

Organized crime? In a small outback town? The two seem incongruous, more something you would associate with the big city, like drug murders and setting fires to tobacco shops. Well, as you can probably guess by my tone, it wasn't really that organized. I just staked out the dog I thought most likely to be at the top of the list as the next target and waited. There weren't that many to choose from. Most people had blue or red heelers, or border collies. After all, this was the outback.

As a rule, the more you paid someone to do a job, the better the outcome you could expect, or the smarter you would think they were. Not in this case. Remember, this was Hopetown.

The funeral director, a slick-haired prick named Ferris, had hired two bumbling brothers as the hapless recruiters for the fights. Hardened kidnappers. Hopetown, the crime capital of the outback west. When it came to Ferris, I didn't see him as much of a threat. After all, he'd been stupid enough to hire the brothers. But a threat he was. And my complacency almost cost me my life.

Two nights into the stakeout, as I sat in my 1975 dark blue Monaro, freezing my balls off—it gets cold out here at night, even in summer—moron one and moron two made their try.

Ferris had sent them out for what he deemed a

worthy opponent for the champion mastiff, who was currently dominating the fighting arena.

Watching their approach, I could but shake my head. Their flashlight was on, of course, and as they moved through the darkness, it was bouncing around like a dancer at a late-night disco.

The brothers stopped and glanced around furtively before going over the paling fence, dressed in black like ninjas out of an '80s martial arts movie. I shook my head again and thought about calling the local police sergeant, Nicole Berger, who just happened to be my partner as well. Possibly not a good idea because she was pregnant, and her eternal morning sickness was evening sickness, and she was likely cuddling the Royal Doulton. That's toilet for the uneducated.

No, it was best that I tackled this one myself.

Now, where was I? Oh, yes, the brothers from Dumb City.

I gave them a couple of minutes before I dragged my frame from the Monaro. The air was filled with the scent of the outback, a dry, dusty smell that often accompanied the nights out here in the west. Mostly from the late after-noon breezes that swept the landscape, picking up the desiccated topsoil as they passed. Then the dust particles remained suspended when there hadn't been any rain for a while. I walked around to the front and sat my butt on the hood. A few moments later, the chaos started.

First came the barking. The deep-throated kind, which could only emanate from the inside of a big dog. Then came the curses. Followed by the shouts and the bleating cries of sheer terror.

Fifty kegs of slavering rottweiler will do that. I wouldn't have been surprised if their jocks were filling with the good stuff.

The flashlight that had been dancing around moments earlier came sailing over the fence like a UFO lighting up the night. It was followed by the first brother, who fell face-first onto the grass verge. That is, if there had been grass there. Instead, small mats of prickles had replaced the grass, as they do during times of drought. The grass dies off and is replaced by hardy weeds. In this case, the good old *Soliva sessilis*, or Bindii. When moron number one came to his feet, his face was a mass of them, resembling a dry beard.

I stared at him, shaking my head. The sight was pitiful. "Dickhead."

Moron number two came over the fence bleeding. His arms were windmilling as he tried to grasp handfuls of air to save himself. Apparently, the dog had gotten a piece of him. He managed to stay on his feet, which meant he didn't suffer the same indignity his brother had.

The slavering beast on the other side of the fence hit it hard. The obstruction seemed to bend with the impact, but fortunately for the brothers, the planks held.

By the time the hapless pair gathered themselves, I was standing in front of them, flashlight in my hand, beam punching them straight in the eyes.

"All right, that's far enough," I snapped with authority.

Staring into the blinding light, the prickle-faced one said, "What are you doing, man? Piss off with the torch."

I thrust the beam closer to his bearded face. "The question is, mate, what are you doing?"

Prickle Face's hand came up to block the stabbing light. "Going home."

"Yeah," said moron number two. "Going home."

I nodded toward the yard. The monster on the other

side was still emitting a guttural growl as it patrolled the fence line. "That way?"

Number one thought for a moment, his mouth twitching beneath the prickles. "Yeah, shortcut. We take it all the time."

"Someone should tell the dog that."

"He was just playing."

Reaching into my pocket, I brought out my cell. The second moron said, "Who are you calling?"

"The police."

"Aw, no man, you can't do that," he moaned.

I glanced up. "Why not?"

"Because I'm bleeding. I have to go to the hospital. I don't have time for all them questions. I could bleed to death." His voice was a whine. "And probably a tetanus shot before I get that lockjaw thing."

The torch dipped as I looked at his wound. Possibly a few stitches would be required. I imagined the doctor scrubbing it clean with disinfectant to kill any germs and smiled. I couldn't help myself.

"What's your name?" I asked.

"Trevor," he replied.

"Shut the fuck up, Trevor," his brother hissed.

"And you?" My gaze was fixed on Moron One. So was the torch beam.

He remained silent, his defiance radiating from every pore on his face.

I said, "All I have to do is ask your brother."

"Tim," he said finally and began picking prickles out of his face, wincing in pain.

I almost felt sorry for him. "Now, here's what is going to happen. You're going to tell me everything, or you can explain it to the police. Choose wisely."

"Tim?" said Trevor. He looked conflicted.

Moron number one glared at his brother. "Shut up, Trev, unless you want to end up in a box."

"But he's got us cold," Trevor whined.

"We were taking a shortcut home. That's all."

"He's not dumb."

"Yeah? Well, bloody one out of the three of us is."

Trevor gave his brother a confused look.

Tim sighed. "Bloody hell. We were looking for a dog."

"Looks like you found it," I pointed out.

He nodded. "You might say that."

"Is it for the dogfighting ring?" I asked them, knowing the answer.

He vacillated for several moments, the battle raging within him swirling vigorously. As hard as he fought it, his lips betrayed him. "Maybe."

"Where do you take them?" I asked, pressing him further.

This time, the silence was longer. I pretended to start dialing again.

"No, wait," Tim interjected.

So I waited for his response, tapping my foot impatiently.

And they looked at each other.

My impatience grew, and I lifted my phone again.

"We are to take it out to Gilford Park," Tim told me.

"Gilford Park?"

He nodded. "Sheep station north of the crossroads. Owned by Linus Barrett. They never have it in the same place twice in a row. The hosts are paid good money to hold them."

I knew the property. "Big gate, large sign, twin stock grids?"

"That's it."

"When is the next fight?" I asked them.

"Tomorrow night," Tim replied tersely.

"Not if we don't get a dog," Trevor said.

"Who runs it?"

"Ferris."

I was taken aback. "The coffin dodger?"

Tim gave me a dumb look. "What?"

With a sigh, I said, "Funeral director."

A nod. "Yeah, that's him."

"Bullshit."

"No bullshit, mate," Trevor said hurriedly as he feared I didn't believe him. "That bastard is scary. Do you know he spent time in Dubbo Jail?"

"Really?"

"Yes, sir. He was inside for beating the crap out of some guy he was hitting up for protection money. The guy never paid. Ferris gave him a warning, and after the second time no money was handed over, he beat the shit out of him."

"He was running a protection racket?" I asked in disbelief. "Ferris?"

"That's what he said," Tim replied. "If you don't believe me, look it up."

"I will."

"Ah, can we go now?" Tim asked.

I nodded. "Yeah, but you've got a busy night ahead of you."

"What?"

"You need to find a dog," I pointed out.

Tim's face fell, prickles and all. "Oh. Yeah. Hold on, you're letting us go?"

"That's right," I said with a stiff nod.

"What if we tell Ferris what happened?" He seemed to get some of his confidence back. So I smashed it.

"What do you think he'll do if he finds out you told me everything?" I asked.

Tim nudged his brother. "He's right. Ferris will take the hide off us. Let's just find a dog."

"There's one over the other side of that fence," Trevor pointed out.

"Fuck that."

CHAPTER TWO

"Hey, Mark," Dolores said as I came through the front door.

This was one of the "other things" I'd mentioned earlier. Dolores was Linda's daughter. I know, right? She kept that quiet, even from Nicole.

The house that came with the sergeant's job in Hopetown was a lot like most Commission homes evident in 1970s suburban Sydney. Three beds, small toilet, shower over the bathtub. The laundry was out the back in a small add-on that the snakes could get into at will. The only thing that varied from fifty years earlier was that the original oil heater had been replaced by a wall-mounted air conditioner. Oh, and an en suite bathroom off the main bedroom. Someone had the forethought to add that.

Glancing at my watch, I then looked at the fourteen-year-old's freckled face, the legacy of her mother's one-night stand with some unwitting Ginger Megs lookalike. "Shouldn't you be in bed? School tomorrow."

She shrugged. "Been doing homework."

"At ten o'clock?"

Dolores rolled her eyes. "Yes, HPE. Something about reproduction and stuff. It's so gross."

Before she could go on, I said, "Don't ask me. I failed."

"Nicole wouldn't say so."

"It's after ten. Bed." I said, not wanting to get into the minutiae of reproduction.

As mentioned earlier, Dolores was the daughter of Nicole's sister, the result of an unwanted pregnancy in her younger years. During a phase of finding out about herself, Linda had become pregnant, choosing to place the child up for adoption rather than suffer the guilt of having an abortion. Then, after all these years, that child had come back into her life. Why? Poor family dynamics. Her adoptive father wasn't there most of the time. Her adoptive mother was an alcoholic who had slipped up one night while on a drunken rampage, revealing the name of her child's birth mother. This had given Dolores a place to start her search for her real mum. She was a good kid, nothing like Linda. Now she was Nicole's responsibility after falling out with her lesbian mother after a shoplifting incident. That's right, I said lesbian. From what I can gather, she'd changed sides after carrying her pregnancy to term and signing away parental rights. Ginger Megs again, I think. Dolores and her mum get along better now than when they had been living under the same roof. Not that I'd know. She had only been with us for a couple of months.

Okay, so she was mine and Nicole's responsibility.

There was movement in the kitchen.

"Hey, sport, time you were in bed," Nicole said, walking into the sitting room. She looked at me and gave me a tired scowl.

"I'm going," Dolores said. She came over and gave me

a hug, then whispered, "She's been barfing up a storm in the toilet."

"I heard that," Nicole said.

Nicole's dark hair was tied in a ponytail tonight. She looked like a wrung-out dishcloth—dark rings around her brown eyes, shoulders slumped with exhaustion.

I walked over to her and opened my arms. She fell into them, and I gently kissed her forehead. "You did this to me," she moaned.

There was no denial from me. "Sorry. But one of the books I read said it should be over soon."

"Great." The sarcasm in her voice was more than evident. She sighed wearily. "At least I don't do it at work."

I nodded. "Sofa?"

"Yes, please."

I sat down while Nicole lay with her head on my lap. We talked about the baby, what we needed to buy, her next birthing class, and about our day. I did, however, omit a few details about mine. As we talked, I stroked the back of her neck, which seemed to make her feel better.

"So you found the dog?" Nicole asked.

I kept stroking. "Yes. The other day."

"Oh."

"I told you that."

"Sorry. Baby brain. So…where to from here?" she asked me.

"I'm following a couple of leads." Which was true.

"Okay."

I broached the subject of our illustrious funeral director. "What do you know about Frank Ferris?"

She frowned as I stroked her hair. "The funeral director? Not much apart from the fact that he buries dead people. Why?"

"I heard today that he'd been in prison before," I told her.

Nicole held her breath for a moment as she contemplated what I'd said. "News to me. I'll look into it."

"News to me too."

"Is he involved with what you're working on?" Nicole asked.

"I'm not sure. I'll find out tomorrow night," I replied. "According to Tim and Trev, he's some sort of criminal mastermind."

"Oh, great," Nicole moaned. "So now the local knuckleheads are casting aspersions about respected businesspeople. According to Tim and Trev, Ronald McDonald is a gastronomic visionary. Oh, crap."

"What?"

She fought back a wave of nausea. "I shouldn't talk about food. What's happening tomorrow night?"

"Not much," I replied evasively.

She turned her head up to look at me. "Mark?"

I gave her my best disarming smile. "It's bedtime."

CHAPTER THREE

Day 2, Tuesday

The following morning, I was greeted by a burning yellow ball of fire clawing its way into the sky to the east. Some fool had left the curtain open again, and after doing battle with a mosquito for the best part of an hour around midnight, there was some effect on my state of mind. I rolled over and found Nicole had already vacated our king-size bed. The only thing I found was her long body pillow. I moaned and said, "I want to stay here."

"What?" Nicole poked her head out from the en suite, toothbrush in mouth. "What?"

"I said good morning."

"What was with you last night?" she asked, waving the toothbrush around as though it were a deadly weapon. "Man, you did some moving around. I felt like I was on a ship in the middle of a cyclone. I'm glad we don't own a waterbed."

"B-52 bomber," I said, referring to the mosquito.

"I don't know how it got in. The windows were shut."

Nicole disappeared again, then reemerged. She came toward the bed in her nightie, her baby bump relatively pronounced. "You know I'm in my second trimester, don't you, Mark?"

"Still?"

"Uh-huh. You know what that means, right?"

I placed my hands over my face and gave her my best Al Bundy impersonation. "Aw, no, Peg, not sex."

Nicole stalked across the bed on all fours and then straddled me. "Don't you deny me, Mark Hayes. Don't you dare. You did this, remember?"

I rubbed her belly. "Well, at least I can't do it again."

She leaned down and kissed me passionately. "You can try."

Climbing from bed twenty minutes later, I pulled on some clothes and left Nicole to shower and get ready for work. Dolores was out of bed and dressed for school. I said, "Morning. Do you want a ride?"

She looked at me and pulled a face. "Yeah, right."

Nodding knowingly, I said, "I get it. I'd be cramping your style."

"Something like that."

I pretended to be hurt. "So this is what I have to look forward to when Gertrude arrives."

"You try naming our child Gertrude and I'll shoot you," Nicole said as she entered the kitchen.

"I thought you were in the shower?"

"I'm a woman, dear. Work it out."

She was dressed in her police sergeant's uniform and looked amazing as always, even if she was showing. I guess it made her all the more attractive. "How about Rosette?"

Nicole stood and stared at me. I shrugged my shoulders. "What?"

She shook her head. "Am I the only adult who lives in this place? Even Dolores is more bloody mature than you."

Seeing trouble on the horizon, Dolores grabbed me by the hand. "Come on. I will take that ride to school."

"I haven't had my toast."

She gave me a hard stare. When she spoke, her teeth were locked together. "Move, or I'll be late."

"Yes, Mum."

It was her way of rescuing me from the wrath of the pregnant woman. I tended to push things a little too far. It was a trait of mine that often got me into trouble. Well, mostly all the time.

As I walked out the door, Nicole called out, "Don't forget to meet me for lunch."

I stopped and looked back. "Where?"

"The pub. It's salad day."

My stomach flipped. Good grief. I hated salad. It was designed to feed cows and rabbits, and I was neither. "See you at twelve thirty."

I closed the door in time to see Dolores walk past the Monaro. "Hey, where are you going?"

"To school," she threw back over her shoulder.

"I thought you wanted a ride," I said.

She stopped, turned, and gave me that *duh* look that teenagers were so good at doing.

With a nod, I said, "I get it. Thanks. See you later."

"Bye."

I grinned wickedly. "You look lovely, by the way."

Not bothering to look back, she gave me the finger.

The morning was already warm, and the growing volume of the cicadas heralded what was to come for the day. Hot, dry, dusty, and annoying.

The door opened behind me, and I turned to see Nicole emerge. "You still here?"

"Uh-huh."

"Nothing to do this morning?" she asked.

I looked at Dolores walking away. "Apparently not."

My phone rang. "Hold that thought?"

Pulling it from my pocket, I answered, "Mark Hayes."

"Mr. Hayes, my name is Eddie Jones. I'd like to hire your services."

His voice sounded distant, possibly a bad connection. Words tumbled from my mouth, probably louder than they needed to be. "How may I help you, Eddie?"

Nicole came in close and kissed my cheek. "See you at lunch," she whispered.

As she did so, I ran my hand down the small of her back and cupped a tight butt cheek. She gently slapped it away and gave me a coy smile. "Behave. People are watching."

I looked across the fence that bordered the front yard and the yard next door. Old Mrs. Hammond was watering her roses, all her attention fixed on us. I gave her a wave and my best smile, hitting the mute button on my phone before calling out, "Morning, Mrs. Hammond. I was just saving the love of my life from a lace wedgie."

Her face paled, and she turned away hurriedly. "Mark, behave," Nicole warned me again.

My phone spoke to me. "Are you there, Mr. Hayes?"

Unmuting, I apologized, "Yes, sorry, Eddie, I'm here. I was distracted by a fox."

Nicole smiled and walked away from me, accentuating the wiggle in her hips as though she were a supermodel on the catwalk in Milan.

"Good. I'd rather not say over the phone. Can I meet with you, say, the day after tomorrow? I have to drive down from Narrabri?"

"Sure, why not. Call me when you get close, and we'll arrange a place to meet."

"Thank you."

The call disconnected. The question now was, what was I going to do for the rest of the day?

CHAPTER FOUR

The pub in Hopetown was one of those grand old buildings with two levels, the verandas all scrolls and fretwork, and four brick chimneys. Built in the glory days of the late 1800s, it was an imposing sight, standing sentinel over the main street. Now, sadly, the second floor was utilized only by the publican and his wife, and the odd occasional paying guest. Gone were the days of full rooms and rough boarders. In its heyday, it had been bursting at the seams with miners from the mine, just like the others. But over time, the miners had taken to either living on-site or been housed in homes. The Hopetown Pub was the only hotel to survive that experience.

As I walked inside through the main bar, I felt several sets of eyes burning into me. I was getting to know some of the locals, but to most, I was the out-of-town guy who got their police sergeant up the duff. Even though Nicole was reasonably new herself, she held a position of trust and was welcomed with open arms.

I stopped at the bar on the way through to the bistro and dining room. It was long and scarred and made of dark hardwood. My entry not escaping the wife of the publican, Giselle stopped her conversation with one of the locals and walked along the bar to where I stood. "What'll it be, Mark?"

"Beer, please, Giselle," I replied. "Schooner of light."

Giselle nodded. In her early forties, she seemed old beyond her years, and used lipstick like it was zinc oxide sunblock. Her hair was graying fast, and she was built like a match with the wood scraped off. As she poured the beer, she asked, "Meeting Nicole here today?"

I nodded and smiled at the mention of Nicole's name. "That's the plan, unless there is a violent bank robbery or a body turns up in the gutter."

She nodded toward the end of the bar where two old-timers were sitting, their half-empty seven-ounce glasses before them. "Don't make jokes about it, Mark. It could happen. Besides, if anyone turns up dead in the gutter, it'll be one of them."

My grin widened. Hector and Frank were old hands in their early eighties. They wandered down to the pub each day for a beer and a chat, reminiscing about the old days when beer was ten cents a glass and cigarettes were twenty cents a pack. Giselle placed my beer in front of me, some of the foam from the head spilling over the side. I thanked her and passed over a ten-dollar note, not expecting much back in return.

"I bet you can't wait for the baby to come along," Giselle said to me, handing over a few coins in change.

"Not as much as Nicole, I don't think."

Giselle nodded. "She looks a little tired. Not going so well?"

I took a sip of my beer. It was cold and bitter and tasted great. "All day sickness."

Her face was suddenly etched with concern. "Poor pet."

"You got that right."

"I remember when my sister was pregnant. She barfed up a storm. By the time she was finished, she was as pale as a ghost. Shocking it was."

"I know the feeling."

She gave me a doubtful look. "Yeah, right."

The dining room was all but empty. Nicole was at our regular table, sipping on a tall glass of water through a black paper straw. She looked up from the menu and smiled as I entered. Placing my beer on the table, I leaned over and kissed her forehead. "I don't know why you're looking at that. You already know what you want."

"It gives me something to read."

Couldn't argue with that. I used to do the same thing. "Fair enough. How is your day going?"

"So far, so good. I have to appear in court after lunch, but the rest of the day should be paperwork. Oh, by the way, I already ordered for both of us."

I forced a smile. "Great, thanks. You really didn't have to."

Horrific images ran through my mind of salad and cold meat spread out across a white china plate. A tear was already forming in the corner of my eye.

I was right. Lunch started out as a somber affair. Anyone who had to sit up to lettuce, cucumber, tomato, beetroot, grated carrot, and a slice of ham for a meal would probably make an analogy of being in a pub at happy hour, with only a dollar to their name. It was bloody heartbreaking.

"Not hungry?" Nicole asked me, devouring her lettuce like a starving rabbit.

I looked at my meal. My eyes rolled from the colors like I was on psychedelic drugs. Shaking my head, I pushed my plate across the table. "Not really. Too much at breakfast. Would you like it?"

"Would I what?" she replied and dragged it the rest of

the way. My fingers lurched back in fear. "You didn't say what you were going to do tonight?"

"Going to a dogfight."

That stopped her massacre of the greenery on her plate. Her eyes narrowed, searching my face to see if I was joking. "You what?"

"I'm going to a dogfight. I have a lead in the case I'm working."

Nicole dropped the fork onto her plate with a loud rattle. I was surprised it didn't shatter under the force of the blow. "You know dogfights are illegal, right?"

"Of course."

"Where?"

"Gilford Park, north of the crossroads."

"You're going alone?" Nicole asked.

"Yes."

She shook her head. "No. I'm coming with you."

I gave her the *duh* look.

She returned it with a hard stare. "What?"

"The last thing I need is Barfing Betty standing beside me while I'm trying to work. You're pregnant, remember? Besides, people know you are a cop."

Nicole picked up her fork and pointed it in my direction. "Call me that again, and I'll stab you in the eye with this fork. Asshole."

I couldn't help it. I grinned.

Her expression softened as another round of hormones kicked in. "Mark, don't."

"You can't come, Nicole."

"It's a police matter, Mark," she pointed out. "I should be organizing a raid."

"Listen, give me a little time, and I'll have everything you need to do just that. I'll even put a bow on it for you."

Nicole shook her head again. "Then take someone with you. How about Paul?"

Paul Wills was her senior constable.

"No, everyone knows him too," I replied.

"Then Suzie or Byron," she suggested. "They're new."

New postings brought new staff. I could see in her eyes that I wasn't going to win. "Suzie."

"Good. I'll let her know when I get back. She can hold your hand."

"You won't get jealous?"

"What?"

"Of Suzie holding my hand. She's quite a looker, you know."

"Don't be a prick."

The smell of cooking potato chips wafted out from the kitchen. I imagined a whole plate in front of me, drowned in salt and gravy and tomato sauce. My stomach growled. Nicole looked up from where she was continuing her meal. "Wow, that was loud."

I shrugged.

One of the bar staff was walking through the bistro at the time, a young lass with dark hair, tattoos, and a sunny disposition, unlike me at that time. Nicole stopped her. "Franky, could you get Jim Rockford here a plate of chips with gravy, please?"

Franky smiled at me. "Certainly."

"You're a doll, Franky," I said to her. "Don't forget the dead horse."

"I know."

"What about me?" Nicole asked, shoveling a piece of beetroot into her mouth.

I pulled a face. "You? You, I can't help."

She blew me a red kiss and kept eating. It was painful to watch. Here was the woman I loved dearly, devouring enough foliage to lay the Amazon bare. All over the world, green groups were gasping in horror.

Ten minutes later, an angel appeared with a feast fit for the gods. With gusto, I hooked into it and demolished the food like a bear wolfing down fresh salmon—I can't believe I compared it to that. Just saying it reminded me of that raw Japanese fish stuff and was enough to turn one's stomach. Horrible.

Nicole leaned back and rubbed her swollen belly. "That was yummy. All I need now is ice cream with a pickle."

I'm glad I finished my meal before she came out with that one. It was enough to turn a man off food for life. I raised an eyebrow.

"What?" she asked.

"You. What kind of a weird combination is that?"

"Shut up, I'm pregnant," she growled at me. "You did it to me, so put up with it."

"If I remember rightly—"

"If you tell me it was all my fault after drinking too much one more time, I'll—"

I held up both of my hands in surrender. "Okay, okay."

"Good."

"But it was."

"Shit, Mark."

"Sorry. Sorry."

"There was one other thing I needed to tell you," Nicole said. "Linda will be here tomorrow. She's staying for a week."

Now I know why she gave in on the chips so easily. I think I mentioned that Linda was Nicole's lesbian sister. She used to be a defense lawyer, still was a ballbuster, and Dolores's mother. Something else I made mention of.

Apart from that, she was quite nice. Although I think she doesn't like me. I can be an acquired taste, just not hers.

"Okay," I said. Then I realized something. "Where is she going to sleep?"

"With me, we've shared a bed a heap of times before."

Which then led to the question, "Where am I going to sleep?"

Nicole smiled at me.

I knew what was coming. "Great. I'm not even in the doghouse, and I get to sleep on the couch."

She pouted at me. "It's only for a week, baby."

"Yeah, we'll see."

And that was the end of that. Nicole went back to work, and I prepared for the evening ahead by going home and falling asleep on the sofa.

CHAPTER FIVE

There was a cool bite in the air that evening. The sun had gone down, leaving a trail of stars in its wake, and with no cloud layer to keep the outback warmth in, the temperature dropped dramatically.

However, in spite of the cold, it was surprising to see how many people were out at Gilford Park for the dogfight when I arrived with Suzie on my arm. A newly minted constable at twenty-two, her blonde hair, normally worn in a bun, was loose and blowing in the breeze. She had pretty features, along with a toughness that reminded me of Nicole.

Growing up in the western suburbs with four brothers, her upbringing had been tough. Upon finishing school, she'd gone in search of stability. The New South Wales Police Force offered her that.

Tonight, she was dressed in tight jeans, a loose top, and a coat, like me. Unlike me, she also carried a gun. "What do you want that for?" I'd asked when I first noticed it.

"I was told to bring it, just in case. Nicole said to shoot you if you did anything stupid. Did you bring yours?"

"I don't carry." Which isn't quite true. I'd been known to use a rifle before.

"Yeah, good luck with that," Suzie snorted.

"What are you doing here?" The question was hissed, panicked.

I turned to see one of the dognappers staring at us wide-eyed, the fear etched on his face. "Where the hell did you think I'd be, Trevor? Darwin?"

"I was hoping," Trevor replied. "Be a lot better if you were."

"Yeah, right."

"Who is she?" he asked.

"My girlfriend," I replied.

He shook his head. "Bullshit. I know her. She's not it."

"It's pretend, Trevor."

His voice was urgent. "You can't be here. If Ferris finds out you're here, he'll kill you and us too."

"You worry too much," I said dismissively.

"Bullshit. He's got four men who ride with him."

Ride with him? He made it sound like a 1950s western. "Where's the fight?"

"In the shearing shed." He looked at Suzie and raised a suggestive eyebrow. "Hey, you're a bit of all right."

I winced. It was pathetic to watch. Suzie crooked a finger, motioning for him to come closer. Trevor leaned in, and she said, "Ever say that to me again, dumbass, and I'll smack you for impersonating a human. After I kick you in the balls."

Trevor glanced at me. I shook my head at him before holding out my arm, and said to Suzie, "Shall we go?"

"Let's."

Trevor licked his lips nervously. "Great. Well, don't say you weren't warned."

There were at least twenty people in the shed. They were gathered around a temporary pen waiting for the fight to begin. Men I expected, but there were more women than I'd envisioned, so there were bloodthirsty onlookers from each sex. The buzz of anticipation was quite electric.

I spotted Ferris talking to a bloke I'd never seen before. At least, I didn't think I had. He was a thin man with gray streaks through his thinning hair, kind of like the actor Bruce Dern. Probably had the same voice as well. I wondered what they were talking about, and then I saw him bend down and pick up a bag. He was a SP bookie. This was far bigger than I had anticipated.

Suzie nudged my arm. I looked at her, and she nodded across the pen to where a large man with a big belly stood. Hal Warner, Hopetown's illustrious mayor, stood there with a skinny blonde woman who wore a cowboy hat. I knew her too. Tracey Curtis.

Only by reputation, mind, not professionally, for she was a woman of the night who worked out of a caravan at the local park and sucked dicks like they were lollipops. In a town where men outnumbered women, she did what some would call a roaring, but illegal, trade. Nicole had busted her recently. I'd been in the station when she'd offered to blow Paul if he let her go with a warning.

Looking up, she caught me staring at her. Pulling on the bottom of her already low-cut tank top, she further exposed a surgically enhanced breast for me to see. With the chill in the air, her pierced rose-colored nipple stood out like a lighthouse beacon on a dark night. Suzie leaned in close and said, "Few dollars there."

"I'd say they've made a few too," I shot back at her.

"You like that kind of thing?" she asked me.

"Can't say as I do. Nicole's milkers will do me just fine."

Suzie punched my arm. "You are mean."

"Just saying, the more natural, the better."

"Like mine?"

She got me. I looked. "Are you trying to get me into trouble?"

Suzie grinned. She was a good kid with a wicked sense of humor, like mine. We were hard to come by.

My eyes skipped around, recognizing a few faces. Then, Ferris climbed into the pen and started to speak. "Ladies and gents, I have some good news for you. Tonight, we're going to do things a little"—his eyes locked on mine—"differently."

Yeah, this wasn't good.

CHAPTER SIX

I became painfully aware of ugly-looking blokes standing on either side of me, crowding my space. Suzie looked back and grabbed for her gun. "No, I don't think you need to do that, love," Ferris said.

A big bloke with broad shoulders stepped forward from behind Suzie and relieved her of the weapon. "Hey, what the hell?"

"Leave it," I said to her, looking around the crowd. "Let's see how this plays out."

Ferris opened the gate into the pen intended for the dogfight. He wore heavy boots with silver studs. Looking at me, he grinned. "Join me, Mr. Hayes."

Glancing around again, I was suddenly overwhelmed by the feeling that I was surrounded by Romans about to watch a gladiatorial fight, their bloodlust evident. I said softly, "Whatever happens, Suzie, do whatever it takes to get out."

"Mark…"

I climbed the low fence, refusing to use the gate, and squared my shoulders. "What now?"

Ferris smiled wickedly and removed his shirt,

revealing a tattooed torso that rippled with muscle. I nodded. "Impressive. You should try out for *Love Island* or some bullshit show like that. Like the prison tats too."

"You're real funny for a bloke about to get the shit kicked out of him," he sneered.

"My dear old grandmother told me once that when you're backed into a corner, don't let them see you're scared. I guess humor is the façade I use." As I spoke, I took off my own shirt. I mean, why not, after all, it wasn't like I was fat or anything. However, if I were playing professional sports, my skin folds would be questionable.

"What now?"

Ferris held out his hand, and someone tossed him a long shovel shaft. "Now we fight," he said with a cold grin.

Another wooden shaft was thrown at my feet. It made a sound like a baseball hitting a bat when it landed on the hardwood floor. I bent down and picked it up, testing its weight and balance. I remembered the Robin Hood story when he and Little John were fighting with sticks on a log across a stream.

"Just so we're clear," I said to him. "What happens if I win?"

"You and the lady get to leave."

"And if I lose?"

"You won't need to worry about that. I'm sure there will be a hole big enough to bury you both in."

"Ferris—" the mayor started, but never got any farther.

"Shut up, Hal. If you don't want to watch, either find a corner where Tracey can suck your dick or leave."

The mayor opened his mouth to speak and then disappeared. I glanced at Suzie, whose face said it all. She was suddenly scared—no, concerned. She looked at me, and I gave her a reassuring smile. What else could I do, right? Besides, how hard could it be, fighting with sticks?

Bloody hard.

Especially when you're not ready for the first assault.

Ferris came at me, swinging the shovel shaft as though he were a knight wielding a broadsword. It came around and struck me across my back because I was standing sideways. Pain shot through me like someone had lit a fire at the base of my spine. I cried out and sank to my knees, dropping my weapon. Then he whipped the piece of cylindrical wood over my head, reversed his swing, and laid it across my guts.

This time, I cried out and doubled over, my arms hugging my middle.

Ferris circled around me and put the wood once more across my back as though he were a ship's master handing out punishment to a troublesome crewman.

As you can tell, I was off to a really bad start.

Ferris hit me twice more.

Sweat washed my face, put there by the intense pain. In the distance, while I concentrated on my own predicament, I could hear the gathered crowd starting to cheer wildly.

Now I was angry, brought on by the lasting pain. I reached out and grabbed the wooden shaft on the ground beside him, looking back at Ferris from where I knelt. He began to circle around me, and I dragged myself to my feet. Man, I hurt, really hurt.

"You're a bit slow there, mate," he said to me, his smile wicked and cruel. "Maybe I should give you a free swing."

Ferris held out his arms and coaxed me forward.

Then, I did the last thing he expected. Using my foot, I broke the shaft. Sometime long ago, I'd been taught to use Escrima fighting sticks. After a while, I'd become quite adept at handling them.

Ferris stared at me curiously. I brought the left half up toward his middle, and Ferris blocked it. As he did so, the right was already moving in a savage backhanded arc, which caught him on the side of the head, splitting flesh and dropping him to his knee.

I moved in closer and hit him again, another solid blow that sounded like a cricket bat smashing into a ball. The blow drew more blood. I went for a third when I was hit from behind. I went down on all fours, pain ripping through my back. I glanced behind me and saw a weaselly-faced customer with a big, shit-eating grin on his face. Ferris was dragging himself to his feet, blood running freely across his face, giving him a ghoulish look. He wasn't as cocky now, just dangerous.

Getting to my feet, I circled around the perimeter of the dueling arena. As I moved past shitface, I lashed out with a stick, catching him unawares and smashing him in the face.

He reeled back and sat down hard, spitting out teeth like they were small pieces of confetti.

Pain still coursed through my body, but my adrenaline was up, and I was far from done. Ferris stared at me, his eyes narrowed with anger. He spat on the shed floor and came at me, rage making him careless. Better for me as I went under the sweeping blow and stabbed hard at his middle with the left stick.

He doubled over, and I brought the right-hand part of the shovel shaft down across the back of his neck. Once more, Ferris went down. This time, it took him longer to move. But I was winning, and I wasn't about to give someone like him a chance.

So I hit him again, and again, and again, and again, and...

"Mark, stop!"

Suzie had appeared beside me, and the crowd had stopped cheering at the sudden violence I had displayed. My body hurt, and I was angry. I stared at her and said, "Let me kill the bastard."

"I can't do that. He's done."

I looked down at Ferris and heard the sirens in the distance. I looked at Suzie. "Nicole?"

"Yes. She wouldn't let it go."

I looked down at Ferris, who was struggling to get up. "Fuck it," I said and kicked him.

CHAPTER SEVEN

"Are you okay?" Nicole asked me after they'd loaded both police vehicles and the ambulance.

I nodded. "Fighting fit."

Until I moved. Then pain shot through my body like 30,000 volts of electricity, and I moaned. Suzie called over. "Sarge, you should get him checked out."

Nicole nodded, placing a steadying hand upon my arm. "I think so. Idiot."

I was only half listening. "What?"

"I said you're an idiot. What if something had happened to you? What happens to me and the baby?"

She had a point. Shaking it off, I said, "I'm fine. If I were any better, I'd be dangerous."

Meanwhile, lightning bolts of pain were shooting through my back, shoulders, and stomach. Okay, so I wasn't that great, but I would get better. Eventually.

"Man, you sure beat the shit out of him," Tim, the so-called smarter brother, called over to me.

"Yeah, the shit," his brother, Trevor, repeated.

"Don't you pair go anywhere," Nicole said, turning her anger on them. "I want a word with you two."

Their faces fell. Tim said, "Can we do it tomorrow?"

"Yeah, tomorrow?" Trev echoed.

"What? Are you pair on repeat?" Nicole asked, shaking her head.

"Shut up, Trev," Tim growled, elbowing him. "Let me do the talking."

Nicole's eyes narrowed. Her finger stabbed at the pair. "Don't bloody move."

She walked away, and the brothers looked in my direction. "She's your missus."

"What makes you say that?"

Tim shrugged. "Just because. And we know her."

I nodded.

"Word is you got her in the puddin' club," Trevor said.

I rolled my eyes. "What the hell? Not like you couldn't tell, Trevor."

"Just saying what I heard."

"Yeah, well, don't let her hear you saying that or she'll ream you in holes you never knew you bloody had."

He smiled, and I could only imagine what was going through his mind. "Just shut up, Trevor."

"Can you get her to let us go?" Tim asked.

I shook my head. "You were nicking dogs for fights. Not only are you in trouble with the police, but the RSPCA will also be so far up your ass that you'll bark every time you open your mouth."

"But you could help, right?" Trevor asked with some enthusiasm.

I stared at him. The guy was as thick as a brick. "Did you hear what I just said?"

His shoulders slumped in resignation. "Yeah."

"Then what part didn't you understand?" I was getting angry. The pain wasn't helping.

"But—"

"Leave it, Trev," Tim said.

Nicole came back. "Give them a ride back to town. I'll send Suzie with you."

"Sure."

"Then go to the emergency at the ambulance center. Get checked out. You look like shit."

"Yes, boss."

Nicole glared at me. She was tired, nauseous, and this was the last place she wanted to be. And she had a long night ahead.

"Come on, Paul, let me blow you, and we'll call it even."

No prizes for guessing who that was. I turned and saw Paul escorting Tracey to the paddy van. I heard him say, "Let it go, Tracey. You've had a lot of things in that mouth of yours, but my penis isn't about to be one of them."

I looked at Nicole. "That woman doesn't give up."

She nodded. "She is persistent. Have to give her that."

"Did you pick up Hal Warner?"

Nicole shook her head. "Haven't seen him."

I grinned slyly. "He must have slipped through the net. Like an eel."

"The man is like Teflon. I'll see you in town."

CHAPTER EIGHT

"Apart from some bad bruising and general soreness, I think you'll be all right," Nurse Gladys said to me.

Her name wasn't Gladys, but I called her that because she reminded me of the matronly figure of Nurse Gladys Emmanuel from the Ronnie Barker show, *Open All Hours*. Plus, I didn't know her name at the time. She was young, large on top and bottom, and what some might call comfortable. I said, "I feel like I've been run over by a truck."

She gave me her best comforting smile. "I'm not surprised with all that bruising. Give it a day or so, and you are going to be all kinds of pretty colors."

I grunted.

She checked my blood pressure again. "That looks fine."

Her touch was light, gentle, and I was thankful for it, especially when she checked around the black and purple bruising for broken ribs.

"The doctor will probably give you some painkillers when he's finished with his other patient," Nurse Gladys said to me.

"The good stuff?" I asked hopefully.

She saw the funny side of the question like a hit-and-run. "I'm sure whatever he gives you will suffice."

Leaving me, she pulled the curtain behind her. Looking at my watch, I noticed it was three in the morning. I lay down, staring at the ceiling. My eyes started to close when I heard a woman say, "They took my daughter, you know?"

Okay, not tired anymore.

"Who did, Ms. Holland?"

"The Kendricks. They had me committed to a mental hospital in Dubbo and then took my child."

"I wouldn't know anything about that, Ms. Holland. I'm just the doctor treating you for a head injury caused by a car accident."

"They did something to my car," she shot back at the doctor. "I went out there to tell them I would get my daughter—my Emily—back."

"Like I said, I wouldn't know about that."

"Well, I'm not going anywhere. I'm staying at the motel, and I intend to stay until I get Emily back." Her statement dripped with defiance.

The curtain shot back, and Nurse Gladys appeared. "Here is a prescription for some medication, Mr. Hayes. You can go home now."

I took it, my mind working, thinking about the woman in the next cubicle. I knew I shouldn't, but I was already hooked, knowing I wasn't about to let it go.

CHAPTER NINE

Day 3, Wednesday

I spent most of the day on the sofa watching the news channel and sleeping. A guy in Melbourne had been caught laundering drug money through one of the casinos, and some bikers had a bit of a fight. There was a drive-by shooting, and two getaway cars had been torched. It was the "done" thing these days. The shooters would steal top-end cars and then burn them once they were finished. Hiring killers was different in the '70s and '80s. Back then, you had your hardened professional killers who did jobs properly. The criminals of today outsourced to what the old-school crims would call hit-and-hopers. Everything was on public display. Back then, when targets disappeared, they usually stayed disappeared.

Dolores came home just after three from school, took one look at me, and said, "You look terrible."

"I feel worse." My words were little more than a tired groan. "How was school?"

"Fine. We had science and biology. Did you know

we're cutting up a frog later this year?"

I winced. "Better you than me."

Dolores shrugged. "Anyway, at least you're still alive," she pointed out.

"True."

"You want anything?"

I shook my head. "I'll be fine, thanks."

"I bet Nicole was pissed."

"Isn't that Aunt Nicole?"

Dolores shrugged. "Whatever. She said I didn't have to call her aunt."

I closed my eyes. "Fine. And to answer your question, she was totally fine."

"Yeah, right. She was far from it when she left here."

I rephrased my statement. "Okay, she was fine when she had someone else to direct her anger at."

"Where is Nicole anyway?" Dolores asked.

I hesitated. "I think she's picking your mother up from the bus."

The mood grew grim. "Right. I forgot."

"How could you forget?" I asked.

She nodded. "Maybe I was hoping her bus would break down. I'll be in my room doing homework."

Twenty minutes later, things took a turn for the worse. Alas, the bus hadn't broken down, and Nicole and her sister arrived home. Nicole came over and gave me a kiss. Linda, on the other hand, gave me a glare. One filled with ice and fire. It's fine that she looked like Nicole, but I was glad Nicole didn't have her demeanor.

"Hi, Linda, still looking lovely as ever. Tongue still sharp?"

She gave me a smile that reminded me of the shark in the movie *Finding Nemo*. "Only for you, sweetie."

Nicole said, "Room at the end of the hall, Linda."

"I'll take my bag down there."

"Give her a hand, Mark."

"I thought camels were good pack animals."

"I can take care of it," Linda said.

Nicole glared at me. It was becoming a habit.

"What?" I asked.

"You could try to be nice, you know?"

"I was." I was in no mood for banter, and I knew Nicole was far from that point too. "All right. I'll try to be nicer. What do you know about the Kendricks?"

She frowned at me. "Own a station south of town. Lionel's Run. Named after the old man who built it up." Now she was suspicious. "Why?"

I told her about the conversation I had overheard while I was in the exam cubicle.

"Never passed my ears before," she said.

I just nodded. "For a police officer with a passion for community policing, you don't hear much, do you?"

"Not when you're concerned. You're a PI. Do your own work." She suddenly looked thoughtful, and her expression changed. "You're not thinking of interfering, are you?"

"Not really," I replied.

"Mark." Her voice was slow, wary. I liked the way her eyebrows knitted together when she got like that.

"It's fine," I replied. "I've got a meeting with a client tomorrow anyway."

Nicole shook her head. "You need more rest." Her concern overrode her suspicion, and her face softened.

"I'll be fine after a good sleep. Besides, I have pills. He's coming down from Narrabri."

"Just don't overdo it."

I smiled. "In Hopetown? Have you seen this place?"

"Not funny. Promise."

"Sorry. I promise."

"What about?" she asked.

"The job? I have no idea," I said truthfully. "He wouldn't tell me over the phone."

Nicole walked over to the fridge and took out a bottle of water. Unscrewing the top, she took a drink.

"Let's hope it is nothing like the last one," she said.

"I couldn't be that lucky." I more than likely could, but left that piece unsaid.

She stared at me doubtfully.

"Point taken, but overall, not that bad."

"What's not that bad?" Linda asked, coming into the living room.

Nicole pointed at me with the water bottle. "Jim Rockford here, and his penchant for getting into trouble."

"He got *you* into trouble, didn't he?" Linda replied. "You can see that."

I opened my mouth to come back with something over the top, but Nicole read my mind. "Stop, Mark. Get yourself a beer and take it outside. Talk to the flies until you calm down."

Maybe it was a good idea. Then I suggested, "Pub for dinner tonight?"

"Sure, why not?"

I stared at Nicole's sister. "You'll like it, Linda. Tonight, witches eat half price."

CHAPTER TEN

The bistro smelled like a multitude of cooked foods, but cutting through it all was the refreshing smell of hot chips. So that's what I had for dinner. Hot chips, steak, pepper sauce, and…

"That stuff will kill you, you know," Linda said with a hint of snark in her voice as Franky put my plate in front of me.

"Thanks, Franky, love. Say, you haven't got some arsenic you could add to the second plate of salad, do you?"

She gave Linda a wary glance. "No, sorry."

"Pity."

Nicole glared at me for the fourth or fifth time since we'd sat down. I was starting to think that if the wind changed, she would stay like that. Old wives' tale, I know.

Looking across at the two plates of salad, I had a mental image of Nicole and her sister with long floppy ears and short fluffy tails. On Nicole, it looked hot, but Linda looked like a prostitute at some brothel that catered to a kinky clientele. I said, "At least I'll die happy. Unlike your husband. Oops, sorry, you don't have one."

Both women glared at me *again,* but I ignored them and went about massacring my meal. Nicole said, "Are you sure you can only stay for a week, Linda?"

"Well..."

Looking up from the slaughter on my plate, I saw Linda staring at me, a hint of evil in her eyes. Oh god, please no. "I might be able to stay for a couple."

Ah shit!

Nicole stared at me, her eyes sparkling with unbridled glee. "That would be good, wouldn't it, Mark?"

I glanced at Nicole and saw the glee suddenly vanish. I nodded. "Yes, wonderful."

"Then maybe I will," Linda said.

It was then that I decided a good option might be to gouge my eyes out with the dessert spoon beside my plate. Something to inflict some pain before...well, you know.

As four more people entered the dining room, I saw the expression on Nicole's face change. It went from one of relative good cheer to being troubled. Of the new arrivals, one was a man in his late fifties, his wife of somewhat the same vintage. There was a young man with them who looked a lot like his father, late twenties, and the last one was a little girl, possibly seven or eight. She had long dark hair and a sunny disposition.

While the others sat at a table, the little girl wandered off to look at a painting on the wall. The older woman said, "Emily, come over to the table, dear."

That was when the penny dropped. I heard Nicole say, "I don't believe it."

"Are they the Kendricks?" I asked her. I'm sure my eyes were as wide as saucers.

At this stage of Nicole's life, glaring seemed to be a favorite pastime. "Leave it alone, Mark."

"I haven't done anything." I raised my hands innocently.

"What is this about?" Linda asked.

Nicole turned to her sister. "Something Mark overheard at the hospital last night."

"You were at the hospital?" Linda asked.

"Not me. Mark. He got a bit knocked around—"

"That I can believe." The sarcasm was loaded thicker than peanut butter on bread. "Remember what happened last time? He got you shot."

I stood up, then groaned when my body protested the sudden movement. "I'm going for a drink."

At the bar, I ordered a beer. While I was there, the younger Kendrick appeared, his daughter in tow. "What would you like, Em?"

"Raspberry, please."

Her father shook his head. "No, too much sugar this close to bedtime."

"Lemon."

"Better, but not much."

The little girl looked up at me. I winked at her. "They say dads are easier going than mothers."

"My mother is dead," she said solemnly.

Suddenly, I looked around for a hole to crawl into. "I'm sorry."

Her reply was innocent. "It's all right. It was a while back now."

I looked at her father, who stared at me for a moment and looked away. I got my drink and went back to the table. Nicole's eyes lingered on my face, knowing that something was wrong. "What is it?"

"The little girl told me her mother was dead."

"Maybe she is," Linda said.

I shook my head. "Something isn't right."

Nicole said, "Be careful, Mark."

"I've got another job tomorrow, remember?" I tried to sound convincing.

"I remember, but just be careful."

CHAPTER ELEVEN

Day 4, Thursday

I got the confirmation call from Eddie Jones the following morning while I was eating breakfast—toast with a thick layer of butter and Vegemite. Was there anything better? If there was, someone kept it for themselves. The butter dripped from the lightly browned bread, and the Vegemite seemed to combine with it.

But here I was at the table.

With everyone else.

Including Linda.

My phone rang. The ringtone, not the one I was used to, was a bloody witch's laugh. I glowered at Dolores, who sat opposite me, beaming. "I'll deal with you shortly."

"Mark Hayes."

"Mr. Hayes, Eddie Jones. I just wanted to confirm that we are on for today?" The road noise in the background told me he was driving and talking on hands-free.

"Sure. Just name a time."

"I should hit town around lunchtime. Should we say one?"

"Sounds good to me, Eddie. There is a truck stop—roadhouse—on the way into town. They serve great food. How about we meet there?"

"Sounds good. See you then."

The call disconnected, and I tossed my cell onto the table in front of Dolores. "Fix it."

With some things, I'm electronically challenged. I'm getting better, but with others I struggle. The phone was no exception. I could use it for certain things. Changing ringtones was not one of them.

Nicole grinned at me while Linda couldn't help but smile. It pissed me off. I asserted my power. "You're grounded for the next week."

"What!" Dolores exclaimed.

"You messed around with my phone," I said. "It is a tool of my work. I can't have it mucked up by silly pranks."

She looked horrified. "I changed the ringtone, not set the bloody thing on fire."

"See, I can be funny too," I replied firmly.

"That's not funny," Dolores pointed out.

"Maybe you'll think twice about doing it next time."

"Grow up, Mark," Nicole said to me.

I raised my eyebrows. "You too?"

"It was a harmless prank. Dolores, you're not grounded."

Shaking my head, I said, "Once again, my authority has been usurped by a female. I can't wait for the addition of another one."

Nicole took a bite of her toast. "You don't know it's going to be a girl, Mark."

"Auntie Mavis said—"

"Wait, who is Auntie Mavis?" Linda asked.

"Someone a lot wiser than you," I fired at her.

"She is good," Dolores said, backing my story... surprisingly.

"Damn it, Mark."

I finished my coffee and climbed to my feet. "Clear the table before school, kiddo," I said to Dolores and scooped my phone from the table. "If that's okay with Aunt Nicole."

"Yes, Dad."

"Don't you ever call him that," Linda snapped.

She smiled at me. "I just thought I'd try it. It sucks."

I nodded. For some strange reason, the savageness of Linda's tone cut. "Don't do it again."

Nicole was dressed in her uniform for work, and I bent down to kiss her. I could taste the raspberry jam on her lips from the lashings she'd put on her toast. It tasted sweet. I moved around to Dolores. She looked up at me and said, "Try it, and I'll stab you with my butter knife."

I rubbed her head. "You love me."

Then I looked at Linda. "You in or out?"

She batted her eyelashes at me. "Try it and find out, sweetie."

A picture of her fangs sinking deep into the flesh of my throat came to my mind.

And I was done.

I moved for the door and had it opened before Nicole caught me. "You're going to see her, aren't you?"

She was good, probably why she was a police officer. "Where would the car from the accident have been taken?"

"It wasn't reported, so it could be anywhere."

I kissed her. "Thanks."

She grabbed my hand before I could get away and placed it on her right breast. I rolled my eyes. "I have a headache, Nicole."

"Bastard."

"The child will be if we don't get married."

Turning and walking out the door, I left her in my wake, stunned. Then she said, "Mark, what do you mean?"

"Bye, babe."

"Mark, tell me what you meant."

"I'll be home later."

"Mark, don't you leave without telling me what you meant."

I climbed into the Monaro and revved the motor. As I backed down the driveway, I had a large smile on my face.

CHAPTER TWELVE

The sign at the Hopetown Motel had seen better days. Letters had faded, others had disappeared, the paint was cracked. As I pulled the Monaro into the parking lot, I saw the manager cleaning the pool. He was talking to another man I didn't know. As I climbed out, the manager waved at me. The stranger looked in my direction and then walked away.

Jarred Fletcher was a thin-faced man who had been in town for a couple of months along with his wife, Alice. They had bought the motel and were trying to bring it back from the brink of death, one room at a time. For the life of me, I had no idea why. Maybe they had money to burn. I'd also met them before on another case.

"Hey, Mark. What's up?"

"I was looking for a customer," I replied. This wasn't my first time.

He wiped the sweat from his brow. "Alice is in the office. She'll help you."

I walked over to the air-conditioned office. As I entered, the chime went off, announcing my arrival. It was one of those high-pitched things that sounded like you were standing on a cat's tail.

A few moments later, the woman in question appeared, emerging from the attached residence through a multicolored streamer curtain. Unlike her husband, who was in his early forties, Alice Fletcher was in her mid-thirties. Her hair was blonde and short. On her arms, she had a multitude of tattoos. Not the sleeve or intricate artwork one usually sees, but the scattered individual drawings that appeared to have been done by a child. She smiled at me. "Hi, Mark. How can I help you?"

"You have a woman here, Alice. Last name is Holland?"

Alice gave me a worried expression. "Oh, Mark, I'm not sure I can give the information out. Sorry."

"She was in an accident. I'm looking into it for her." It was a lie, and perhaps I would be judged for it someday, but today wasn't that day.

"You are working for her?" Alice asked, her demeanor changing.

"Yes."

"Why didn't she tell you her room number?" she asked.

I shrugged. I was damned to hell. I could feel it. "I don't know. She had a head knock."

"She's in room six."

"Thanks, Alice. I'll dance at your wedding."

She smiled at me. "Bit late for that, I'm afraid."

I left the office and walked under the steel awning along the line of rooms until I reached the right one. I knocked.

"Who is it?" The door between us made her sound miles away.

"Mark Hayes."

"I don't know you. Go away."

I waited a moment and said, "I'd like to talk to you, Ms. Holland, about Emily."

There was a drawn-out silence, and then the door opened, the security chain in place. I can't understand the point of them, really. Once the door was open, a good kick, and it was all over. I waited for her to look me over and speak.

"What about Emily?" she asked. There was concern on her face.

"Can I come in, please?"

"No."

"I overheard you at the hospital," I explained. "I was in the cubicle next to yours. I wasn't listening in but... well, you know."

"I don't know you, Mr. Hayes."

I took out my ID. "I'm a private investigator. My partner is the local police sergeant. If you want, you can give her a call. She knows I'm coming here."

"Hey, Mark, is everything all right?" Jarred called over to me.

I waved back. "All good, Jarred."

The woman looked at me again. She closed the door, and I heard the chain rattle. Then she opened the door properly and stepped aside. "Come in. I don't want them watching."

"Who?"

"The owners. There's something wrong with them. They're not right."

"Okay."

I went inside. The woman was in her late twenties, with dark hair and a small white sticky plaster on her forehead. Her wild eyes seemed to settle down after a moment, and I waited for her to calm. I said, "I'm sorry to spring this on you, but I heard your...part of your story, and I thought maybe I might be able to help."

Her eyes widened and started their dance again. "You can get my daughter back?"

No. "I can't promise that. How about you tell me what happened from the beginning, and I'll see if I can help at all."

"I cannot pay you." It was a statement. "God knows I can barely pay for this place."

I held up a placating hand. "I haven't asked you to, Ms. Holland."

"Call me Grace," she said.

"Okay. Grace, you call me Mark. Now, start at the beginning. Why is your daughter with the Kendricks?"

"She is their granddaughter," Grace replied. "Tyrone, their son, was my husband. Her name is Mabel and his is Henry. They are the most evil people."

"Why is that?"

"They had me committed to a psych ward in Dubbo while they took me to court and got sole custody of my Emily."

"Why?"

"Pardon?"

"Why were you committed?" I asked. "Were you a danger to yourself? To others? To your daughter?"

A myriad of emotions crossed her face. "No. No! It was the only way their son could get custody of my daughter because I had left him."

"Why did you leave him?"

"Because he used to beat me," Grace replied vehemently, her eyes flaring. "Isn't that enough? One day, I woke up and decided I'd had enough and left, taking Em with me."

"Okay."

"He was going to kill me," she said suddenly. "I could tell by the way he looked at me."

I nodded. "Did you go to the police?"

"Yes. And they believed me at first," she replied.

"At first?"

"The Kendricks hired a lawyer and started to turn things back on me, saying that I did all the injuries to myself. They filed to have my daughter removed from my care because I was a danger to her, and a restraining order was put on me." I could hear the despair in her voice.

"An AVO?"

"Yes."

Grace walked over to a small bench and picked up a packet of cigarettes. She took one out and placed it between her lips. She fluffed around for her lighter and looked at me. I pointed at the small no smoking sign on the wall.

Taking the cigarette from her lips, she put it back in the packet.

"Then what happened?" I prompted.

"My case was about to go before the court when somehow theirs was pushed up. The magistrate happened to be a friend of the family. The hearing lasted five minutes, and the outcome granted them full custody of Emily, and I was committed to psychiatric care for six months."

"Have you seen your daughter since?" I asked.

"No." She paused before continuing. "Do you have any idea what it's like living with crazy people all around you? They load you up on drugs and get inside your head. I was fine when I went in, but I'm not so fucking sure now."

The battle within me raged as I tried to decide whether to mention the next piece of news. Then, before I could make up my mind, it was out. "She seems to think that you are dead."

Looking back now, it was a mistake. A horrified expression came over her face. "No! It can't—I have to see her."

Maybe I should have kept that part to myself. "Wait. It won't help."

"She must know I'm still alive."

"Tell me about the accident."

"What?"

"The car accident," I prompted.

"I...I was out there, at Lionel's Run. They took me inside, but they refused to let me see Emily. I left and, on the way back to town, I lost my brakes. The car went into a ditch, and I hit my head."

I nodded. "Will you promise me that you won't do anything until I look into it?"

"I...I suppose so."

"Thank you. Do you have any pictures or evidence of the beatings?"

"My solicitor in Dubbo has them. Can you really help me, Mark?" Grace said.

I thought of Linda, then lied. "Yeah, I reckon there might be a way."

There was a knock at the door. I glanced at Grace. "You expecting someone?"

"No."

She opened the door, and a familiar face stood on the other side of the opening. "Grace Holland?"

"Yes."

"I'm Senior Sergeant Nicole Berger of the Hopetown police. I—"

"What's up?" I asked.

She looked at me and said, "This has nothing to do with you, sir. Please remain quiet."

"But—"

"Step outside, sir."

I looked into Nicole's eyes and could see there was no give in her. I walked past Grace. "Tell them nothing."

Out in the parking lot, Suzie was waiting. She said to me, "How are you feeling?"

"I hurt," I replied. "What is this all about?"

"The woman still has an AVO on her. We've got two choices. Lock her up or give her a warning."

"How's the birthing suite this morning?" I asked, trying to gauge which way this was about to go.

Suzie stared at me, her eyes smiling for her. "You are awful. But she's fine."

I waited for Nicole to finish. Nicole then walked over to where we stood. "You should stay away from this, Mark."

I shook my head. "She's told me enough to make me curious."

"These people have connections and history."

With a nod of acknowledgment, I said, "I know, Nicole. But something is off with all of it."

"Damn it, it's all off," she hissed quietly. Her eyes blazed.

"They told the girl her mother was dead," I said curtly. "It's all wrong, and I'm looking into it."

Nicole rolled her eyes in exasperation. "Fine. Just be careful. I'm not about to lose the father of my child because of some crazy bloody…"

"I will. Is your sister at home?"

"You leave her out of this," Nicole growled.

"If I'm going to jail, sweetheart, I'm taking her with me," I growled with a heavy American accent.

"Mark—"

"I just want to ask her a legal question. That's all."

Nicole poked me in the chest with a straight finger.

"You get her involved, and I'll castrate you, Mark Hayes."

"Okay."

"With my teeth."

Now, that was something to look forward to.

CHAPTER THIRTEEN

I talked some more with Grace, found out where the vehicle went, and then headed home. I still had a couple of hours before my meeting with Eddie Jones, which allowed me to check in with Linda. When I arrived, she was sitting on my bed watching some kind of reality show. She hit the off button on the remote and said, "I don't know how people watch mind-numbing shit like that."

"You got a moment?"

"Nicole said not to listen to you," she said abruptly.

"She called you, huh?"

Linda nodded stiffly. "She did."

She picked up what looked to be a crossword or a word search book. "Okay," I said and turned away.

She sighed. "So...what is the problem?"

I relayed to her what I'd been told. She remained silent until I was finished and said, "Leave it with me."

"What?"

"I will get the file from her solicitor in Dubbo and look it over. Then I'll make a few inquiries about the judge who was presiding over her case."

"Are you sure you want to get involved, Linda?"

"It'll give me something to do. Call me a research assistant. Besides, I may not like what you do, but you have a good heart, Mark. You proved that with Dolores."

I took it as the compliment that it was meant to be and thanked her. "One more thing, could you smooth it over with Nicole? She's going to be pissed at me getting you involved. She threatened to castrate me with her teeth."

"I'll take care of it."

"Nicole or the castration?"

She smiled at that, not the wicked smile I was used to.

Leaving it at that, I headed back out into the heat of the day and fought the swarms of flies on the way to the Monaro. When I climbed in, I burned my hands on the steering wheel. Cranking the AC up to max, I waited for the oven to cool slightly before backing out onto the street, then headed to where Grace's vehicle had been taken—Bonner's place.

The Monaro came to a stop in the gravel and dirt parking lot outside the secondhand car yard. Rod also doubled as a mechanic's garage. He saw me coming. We'd not hit it off when I moved to town, arguing over the price he tried to charge me when servicing the Monaro. I think it would depend on how he was feeling on the day. I knew it was going to be bad the moment he emerged from his office with a square of sticking plaster on his jaw.

"What do you want, Mark?" he growled.

At least he still had his barbed-wire tongue. "You been fighting?"

"No, fucking skin cancer. What do you want?"

"How the hell do you get skin cancer there?"

"Don't ask stupid questions," he replied.

Shit. "Car was in a wreck. It was brought in here."

Bonner nodded. "Really? I thought it would have been your missus that came to see me about it, actually."

Now I was a little more interested. Little alarm bells started to ring in my head. "There something wrong with it?"

He nodded. "Yeah, Jimmy found something unusual."

"Like what?"

"Brake line had a hole in it," Bonner said.

"A rock or something?" I asked, knowing what the state of the roads was like around the district.

Bonner turned and called toward the garage. "Jimmy, get out here."

A thin, dark-skinned young man with curly black hair appeared, wiping his hands on a dirty rag. "What is it?"

"Tell Mark what was wrong with that brake line."

"It was cut," Jimmy informed me.

"All the way?"

The young mechanic shook his head. "No. Just enough for it to leak out and cause the accident."

"Are you sure?" I asked.

"Of course he's bloody sure," Bonner growled. His face softened. "How's the Monaro running?"

I nodded. "Runs like a baby."

"Couldn't sell you something else? Huh? I've got a great Land Cruiser out there. Only fifty grand."

"No."

"Is there anything else?"

"Just to clarify it," I said to Jimmy. "Could it have been anything else other than a cut?"

"No."

"How much more do you have to do to it?"

"Guard, bumper, new radiator. Best part of a week. You know how things are out here. It's wait-a-week country."

He was right. If you wanted anything not in stock, you had to wait a week.

"Thanks." I looked at my watch. It was time to meet Eddie Jones. If I thought life was tough already, it was about to get worse.

I climbed into the Monaro, and my cell rang. Screeched like a witch, actually. Dolores still hadn't fixed it. It was Linda. How appropriate.

"Mark, I got the lawyer in Dubbo to send over what she has. She told me that Tyrone Kendrick is a serial offender. What's more, she called him dangerous."

Just what I needed. "What do you mean, serial offender?"

"Assault on a kid at school. Went away with money. Another assault, this time on a woman at agricultural college. It went away too. Mum and dad's money."

I said in a low voice, "Anything else, Linda?"

"Not yet. I'm making some inquiries about the magistrate."

"Thanks, you're a lifesaver."

"I know."

I decided to tell her about the crash. "You'll like this. The accident was caused by a partially cut brake line."

"Christ," Linda snapped on the other end of the call. "I was thinking that to have been able to do what they did, there must be a link somewhere with the magistrate. Maybe way back. I'll run that down."

"Just don't make waves for yourself, Linda."

"Ha!" she exclaimed. "I have someone in Sydney who does that for me."

"An investigator?"

"The best."

The call disconnected, and I started the Monaro. Then I headed for the roadhouse on the edge of town.

CHAPTER FOURTEEN

The heat radiating off the concrete apron at the roadhouse was intense. It had been soaking up the rays since early morning, and with the sun now at its zenith, it was thrusting them back at whoever dared to cross it. I parked the Monaro and ran the gauntlet across the heated expanse to the roadhouse café, my boots crunching on the grit deposited by countless trucks and cars. There were three rows of gas pumps out front, with an additional two of diesel at the side beneath a large awning where trucks could pull in.

As the automatic doors opened, cool air rushed to embrace me, and I enjoyed the respite from the oven outside. I walked over to the counter, a row of candy on one side and magazines and papers on the other. I was greeted by a woman with red hair, freckles, and a love of life the size of herself. "Hey, Mark, what'll it be today?"

"Burger without the lot, Jasmine," I said.

I know what you're thinking. How do I know so many people in town when I haven't been there that long? The answer is simple. The job. While I waited for business to pick up on the PI side, I delivered flyers for the local supermarket into letter boxes. You get to meet a lot of people that way and see a lot of things. Some you wish you could unsee. It was something I still did today, every two weeks on a Thursday. Hey, I'm not a proud man, and it brings in some dollars. We have a baby on the way, after all.

She smiled a broad, gap-toothed smile. "Burger, chips, and hold the salad."

"You're a gem, Jasmine."

"No worries, love. You want some of them too?"

My eyebrows shot up. "Potato gems?"

"Sure."

A broad grin split my lips. "Don't let Nicole hear you talk dirty to me like that. She'll get jealous."

She gave a dismissive wave. "I'd give her a run for her money, sweetheart."

My smile widened.

"Say, anyone new in at the minute?" I asked.

"Meeting someone?"

I nodded. "Yeah. Client."

"Business is booming, huh?"

I nodded. "So much so that I'll see you on my round next week."

She nodded over my shoulder. "Sitting down, the back corner. Came in about ten minutes ago. Tracey is with him. He'll need rescuing."

I rolled my eyes. "Thanks, Jas."

"No worries, I'll bring it over when it's ready."

My next mission was to extricate Eddie Jones from the clutches of Tracey. I hurried to the table where they sat, and she looked up at me. "Go away, pirate. I'm working."

Wearing her trademark low-cut top, her breasts billowed upward, exposing their milky-white flesh and the top of a lacy red bra. I took twenty out of my wallet and stuffed it down in her cleavage. I grinned at the butchering of the name. "It's Poirot, and I'm working too."

She looked up at me and could see that I was serious. She stood up and touched my arm. "You know, I could give you a discount, Mark. In which case, that twenty would get you a taste."

"You're too much woman for me, Tracey," I said. "Besides, I don't like chewing gum."

She winked at me as the insult went over her head. "Just remember me when your woman is eight months along and can't stand to be around you."

She left, and I stared at the man across the table. He had light-colored hair and a relieved expression on his face. He looked to be mid-thirties. "Eddie Jones?"

He nodded. "Yes. That's me."

I held out my hand to shake. "I'm Mark Hayes. I believe you want to hire me."

CHAPTER FIFTEEN

"I want you to find the person who murdered my father."

We finally got there. It took a while, but here we are.

I adjusted my position in my seat, wincing at the pain ricocheting around my body, the obligatory aftereffects of having taken such a beating at Gilford Park. Jones looked at me, a puzzled expression on his face. "Are you all right, Mr. Hayes?"

I nodded. "Hazard of the job. Call me Mark."

"Fine, Mark."

"Before we go any further, how did you find out about me?" I asked. A man has to know if his advertising dollar is working or if he's wasting his money.

"A friend recommended you. You did some work for them in Melbourne."

"Name?"

"Carol Winters."

The filing cabinet inside my mind opened, and I sifted through the locked files until I encountered hers. Carol Winters was a middle-aged woman whose husband was having an affair. A domineering, abrupt woman, she didn't care who was offended when she opened her mouth. I followed him around for a couple of days, took pictures, and that was it. Just bread and butter stuff, but she paid well. "Nice lady."

"She's a bitch," Eddie replied bluntly. "But she's also a friend."

I nodded. "Now, what's this about your father? When did the murder take place?"

"Around thirty years ago," Jones replied.

Holy shit, was this guy serious? "Thirty years ago?"

"Yes, I was five at the time."

"How do you know it was murder?" I asked him. "Don't take this the wrong way, Mr. Jones—Eddie—but thirty years is a bloody long time."

He nodded. "I know it is. But from what I know, I'm convinced it was murder. Even though the ruling was accidental death."

I sighed. "You'd better fill me in so I can make a decision."

"My father was out riding the dams on our property when he supposedly fell off his horse, hit his head, and was found in a dam. There was a storm at the time."

"Sounds plausible."

Jones's face hardened. "My father had been a professional rodeo rider. He knew how to ride. He wouldn't just fall off."

"It has been known to happen. Horse saw a snake, got skittish. Lightning strike, thunder." I held my hands apart, gesturing.

"Not to my father." Jones was adamant. "He had to have been knocked off his horse. Murdered."

I nodded once more. "Are you going to be around town for a while?"

"Yes."

"Fine. Give me a day or so to look into it, and I'll get back to you. What was his name?"

"Les Jones."

"Fine."

Eddie reached for his wallet. "How much do you want?"

Holding up a placating hand, I said, "We'll worry about that if I take the job."

Eddie thanked me and then left me there to eat my lunch. I could have asked him more questions, but I wanted an unbiased opinion of the death. The window where I was seated looked out at the gas pumps. I'd just shoved another mouthful of burger deep into my gaping maw when I saw a white 4x4 pull up. As I watched, Tyrone Kendrick got out. He was alone and began to fill the tank of his Land Cruiser.

Then, from nowhere, Grace Holland appeared.

"Ah, shit," I growled around the mouthful of burger. I lurched to my feet and headed toward the door. "I'll be right back, Jas."

I hate hot weather. Coming from inside where the air conditioning was cranked up, it was like walking into a bloody wall, and it tried to slap you down. Then, flies came from nowhere in swarms, and I was hesitant to open my mouth.

I could hear the voices before I even got close. The pair of exes were yelling at each other, faces red. But not from the heat. Then I saw Tyrone lift his hand, about to strike.

"Hey!" My voice cut through the heat of the Hopetown day.

They both looked at me.

"You'd better rethink what you're about to do, mate," I cautioned him. My eyes had narrowed to slits.

"Get her the fuck away from me. The crazy bitch has an AVO out on her. I'm only defending myself."

"Maybe it should be the other way around," I growled. "From what I just witnessed."

"I told you," Grace said with a raised voice. "You saw it. He used to beat me all the time."

Grabbing her by the arm, I escorted her out of earshot. "What the hell do you think you're doing? Do you want to end up in jail?"

"I—"

"No, I don't want any excuses," I hissed. "Go back to the motel. For the life of me, I have no idea why you are here. If he goes to the police, they'll lock you up this time."

"I was out for a walk, and I happened to see him."

A walk? Who goes for a walk in stifling heat like this? "So you thought it would be a good idea to confront him for all the world to see? Is that it?"

"I wasn't thinking."

I could understand why she did it, and I probably would have done it myself if the roles were reversed, but she was walking a fine line where one slip could put her behind bars. My expression was grim. "I'll say you weren't."

"But I want my daughter back."

"It won't happen this way. Now, go back to the motel."

Her shoulders slumped. "Fine."

"If you need to talk to me, you have my number."

I watched her walk away and then turned to stare at Kendrick. He saw me looking. "What?"

I shook my head and went back inside. The last thing I needed was more trouble. As I paid for my meal, Jasmine asked, "You headed to the rodeo?"

"Tomorrow night?"

"Uh-huh."

"Maybe. Depends on the boss," I told her.

"Tiger Smith is bronc riding," Jas informed me. "Should be good to watch."

Tiger Smith was the runner-up Australian bronc riding champion in 2023. He hailed from Hopetown, or rather, a station outside of it. "I guess I'd better go then."

"See you there."

CHAPTER SIXTEEN

When I arrived at the police station, I found Nicole there on her own. She came out of her office when I entered and looked in my direction. "You either want something or you're here because you miss me. I'm thinking you want something."

Moving behind the counter, I wrapped my arms around her as best I could and kissed her on the lips. "I want you, of course."

She sighed, knowing I had just lied to her. "I'm sorry about this morning. I felt like shit."

Kissing her again, I replied, "That's okay. I probably could have handled it better."

"Why are you here?"

"How would I go about finding information from thirty years ago?" I asked her.

"No, Mark."

"Babe?"

She pushed me away, her loving demeanor now gone. "Don't fucking babe me, Mark. You want to find something from thirty years ago, try the newspaper."

I held up my hands in mock surrender. "All right, all right, I'll do that."

"Is there anything else you want?"

"Would you like to accompany me to the rodeo tomorrow night?" I asked.

Nicole smiled. Her anger vanished. "Are you asking me on a date?"

I grinned. "It would be if your sister didn't come. Or Dolores."

She came in close and kissed me. "You're awful. But Dolores is already going with her friends."

"Since when?"

"Since she asked me."

"She didn't mention it to me."

"Because she likes me more," Nicole said with a wry smile.

The door opened, and Suzie walked in, Byron in tow. The latter had a large dollop of barbecue sauce on his shirt. Opening my mouth in mock horror, I said, "Oops. Mama not issuing bibs to the kiddies no more?"

He rolled his eyes. "There would be no oops if Danica Patrick knew how to drive."

Suzie giggled. "If you knew where your mouth was, you wouldn't have that problem. Who's Danica Patrick anyway?"

Byron rolled his eyes. He said, "Former NASCAR driver."

"Oh."

Nicole said, "Get a clean shirt, Byron. Then take the Land Cruiser over to Bonner's to get the taillight fixed."

"Yes, boss."

Suzie held a finger in the air as she suddenly remembered something. "Oh yes, the woman wasn't at the motel either."

My ears pricked. "What woman?"

"Your friend," Suzie replied. "We got a report that she was seen arguing with Tyrone Kendrick at the roadhouse."

Bloody shit!

"She wasn't at the motel when we went looking for her."

Nicole stared at me. She could see the concern on my face and knew there was something I hadn't mentioned. "Any idea where she might be?"

I shook my head. My voice went high-pitched. "No."

Which was true. The last I knew, Grace was headed back to the motel. I made a mental note to check on her later. She should have gone straight back. So God only knew where she had gone.

"I'm off," I said and kissed Nicole. "I'll see you tonight."

"Stay out of trouble."

"You know me."

"Yes, I do. That's why I said it."

CHAPTER SEVENTEEN

Having had the foresight to park under a tree, the Monaro wasn't as hot when I returned to it. I drove around the block to the Hopetown Herald to continue my investigation of Les Jones. I angle-parked my chugging beast and climbed out after switching the motor off.

If there was one thing I hated more than heat, it was flies. And more than flies, it was journalists. But Larry Nelson was different. Kind of.

There was a moment of hesitation as I stared at the glass front doors, working up the courage to enter. He was annoying in every sense of the word, but there was something about him. He was a good source of information.

Larry was seated behind his desk, typing at his computer. He looked up at me through tired eyes and black-rimmed glasses that resembled the bottom of Coke bottles. "Here he is, Hopetown's own Cliff Hardy. Should I hold the front page?"

The paper only came out twice a week and consisted of about five pages. So the front page was a big deal. The last publication was plastered with Tiger Smith coming to ride in the rodeo. Shaking my head, I said, "I would have thought you had too much already."

"You sure give a good journalist plenty of fodder," he replied. "Do you have any comment about what happened?"

"No."

He picked up a camera. "Can I get a picture of your bruises?"

"How the—no, Larry."

"Come on, Mark, give me something."

"How about, 'Local mayor seen with lady of the night at illegal dogfight?'"

He looked excited. "You're not playing with me, Mark, are you?"

"No, Larry, he was there. But by the time the police showed, he'd vanished like the phantom he is. Come to think of it, he's pretty much like that all the time. When was the last time you saw him?"

He ignored the question. "Excellent. I'll save that for the next go-around."

"Then it'll be old news."

"You're right. Maybe I need a special edition. What can you tell me?"

"Depends on what you can tell me, Larry," I replied.

Like me, Larry had come from the city. He, however, had moved across the border from Melbourne, somehow finding his way to Hopetown. His former employer was a tabloid that had shut down due to the lack of hard-copy sales. He'd been their crime reporter and, by all accounts, had broken a few hard cases in his time.

And like I said, he was good for information.

He stared at me. I said, "About thirty years back, there was a death ruled accidental. You got any information on it?"

"Shit, Hayes, that's well before my time. And from what you just told me, well…"

"Don't you have a store or something?" I asked.

"Come with me."

He got up from his seat and walked to the back of the building. He opened a door and said, "That's the archive. Go for it."

I walked forward and stopped dead. "Bloody hell."

The room was lined with shelves and smelled musty. Each shelf had a year marked on it, which narrowed it down some. I took a deep breath and said, "I guess I'd better get started."

"Before you do," Larry said. "What else can you tell me about the other night?"

Not one to knock back an opportunity when I saw one, I said, "You help me, and I'll help you."

"But I just did."

I shrugged. "I'll let you take a picture of my bruises."

"Bloody hell, Mark, you're a hard man."

So we went to work together, and an hour later, I was looking at a paper with an article detailing what had happened. Apparently, Les Jones had been out riding boundaries and checking dams and windmills on their property, like his son had said. He'd fallen from his horse and hit his head before being found in the dam. Accidental death. What it also told me was that the body was found by his friend, Ike Smith.

I looked over at Larry. "Ike Smith. Any relation to Tiger?"

The newspaperman nodded. "His father. According to people I interviewed for the Tiger story, the old man was a good bronc rider himself. Apparently, he and Les Jones had the rodeo circuit nailed down between them. He never went back on the circuit after Les died. Said it wasn't the same without him."

"How old is Tiger?" I asked curiously.

"Twenty-eight. Ike's second wife. His first wife died a year after Les did. A bull got her in the yards. Ike sold all his cattle after that and went into sheep."

"How do you know all this?"

Larry stared at me. "I'm a journalist."

"I don't suppose the doctor who filled in the death certificate is still around?"

"Doc Elias Rendado. Sure, he lives over on Hooper Street."

I nodded. "Thanks, Larry."

"You going to tell me what you're doing?"

"Eventually."

As I walked out the door, he called after me, "Hey! What about the other night? And the pictures?"

I stopped. "You're a journalist, journalize."

He stared at me.

Shit.

CHAPTER EIGHTEEN

Dr. Elias Rendado was in his early sixties now, retired, and had taken up fishing until the river ran dry. Now he milked snakes. He was in the middle of wrangling a mulga snake, or king brown, when I arrived. Just seeing the big serpent made my blood run cold. The body was thick, muscular, and the eyes black and mean. It was enough to give a man nightmares. The room was filled with glass-fronted cases where he kept them. I could feel them watching me, just waiting for their chance to give me an excruciating death.

"I don't know how you can do stuff like that," I said, staring at the snake.

Rendado gave me a wry smile. "I'm due to give it away. I'm not as quick as I used to be. One day, I might get tagged if I'm too slow."

"Just don't let it go, or you'll have a Hayes-sized hole in your wall."

Rendado smiled. "What can I do for you, Mr. Hayes?"

"Are you sure you want to talk while you're doing that?" I asked and looked around his snake room at the other glass cages again. "I'm happy to wait."

"Okay."

"How many do you have?"

"Venomous?"

"That'll do."

"They're all venomous. Fifteen."

I shivered and waited for him to finish.

When he was done, he put the reptile back in its enclosure. He held up the glass jar with the venom in it and said, "The mulga snake might not be as deadly as the eastern brown or taipan, but they make it up by being able to pump in a large amount of venom."

I swallowed hard. Many a night, my dreams had been haunted by snakes chasing me. My feet mired in treacle, unable to move fast, the damn things always bite you. "I'll take your word for it."

He smiled at me, his wrinkled face becoming like a map with rivers marked on it. "Shall we go out onto the veranda?"

"That might be best," I replied, looking and feeling relieved.

As I walked past one of the glass cages, a snake struck out, an audible thump being heard. Rendado said, "That's Oscar. He gets a bit grumpy on milking days."

"I'm not surprised."

"I usually milk them of a morning. I find my reflexes sharper then. Never of an evening." Once we were outside, he asked, "What was it you wanted again?"

"Thirty years ago, you signed the death certificate of Les Jones."

Rendado nodded. "I examined the body too."

This was a turn-up for the books. "It was ruled an accidental death."

He nodded. "That's right."

"Was there anything off about it?"

The doctor looked puzzled. "Why?"

"His son wants me to look into it. He believes that his father was murdered."

His eyebrows shot up. "Eddie is here?"

I nodded. "Yes."

"Good lord, I haven't seen that boy in a long while. Not since the property was sold."

"You know him?"

Rendado smiled, remembering. "Sure, I was the family physician."

"What can you tell me about his father?" I asked.

"Would you like a cold drink?" Rendado asked before continuing.

"What have you got?"

"Water or Coke."

"Coke would be great."

"Be right back."

He disappeared inside. From where I was seated, I could see around his front yard. It was green from being watered, and the garden was filled with roses and other flowering plants. Rendado returned a short time later and passed me one of the two cans of Coke he held. It was already becoming layered in condensation, and a large drip broke free of the bottom and landed on my shirt, leaving an almost perfect wet circle.

"Now, where were we?"

"Les Jones," I prompted.

"Ah, yes. Brilliant rodeo rider. Some say he was part of the horse when he rode. I remember the other side."

"What side is that?" I asked.

"Patching him up. Many times, he came home with broken ribs or some other injury inflicted by being thrown."

"Why not get fixed where he was?" I asked curiously.

"Because I was the only doctor he trusted." A dirty 4x4 went past on the street, a hole in the exhaust making it sound like an old chaff cutter. Rendado had paused because of the noise. "They brought him in the day after it happened for me to examine."

"They didn't do a crime scene out there just in case?" I asked.

"This was thirty years ago. Hopetown was a different place, and they did things differently. Besides, I was told that it was an accident, and they just wanted confirmation on it."

"You never found anything that said otherwise?" I asked.

"No. Everything pointed to him falling and drowning. There was a bruise and cut on top of his head, and he also had a fractured skull where he'd hit."

"Water in the lungs?"

"Oh, no, he didn't drown. They pulled him from the dam, but the fall where he hit his head was what killed him."

I took my hat off and said, "Could you show me where? If you remember, that is."

The doctor stood up and came over, touching me on top of the head. "About there."

I put my hat back on. "Thanks."

"Is there anything else you want to know?"

Shaking my head, I said, "No, I think that about covers it." Then I thought and said, "Yes. Why the snakes?"

"About twenty years ago, I had a little girl brought in after being bitten by a mulga snake. She died because we didn't have antivenom. So I made a pact with myself that no one in Hopetown would die of a snakebite again. After that, I started handling and milking them. Everything gets sent to the city. They send the town a supply of anti-venene. No one in this district has died from a snakebite since."

I smiled at him. "Give it away, Doc. You've done your bit."

He returned my smile. "One day."

CHAPTER NINETEEN

I sat in the Monaro with the air conditioning running. It was about the coolest place to be for the time being, and it wasn't that cool. I dialed the number I had for Eddie Jones and waited for him to answer.

"Hello?"

"Eddie, Hayes. Listen, I've done some preliminary work, and I have to agree with the report. It looks to be an accident."

There was a disappointed silence on the other end.

Continuing, I said, "I talked to Doc Rendado, and he was of the same opinion."

"Rendado was wrong. He was wrong then. He is still wrong."

I decided to humor him. "Who was it?"

"What?" There was confusion in his voice.

I said, "You seem set on it being murder. Who do you think did it?"

He hesitated. "The mine."

"The mine?" I asked.

"Peak Vale Copper. A year after the place was sold,

copper was found on it, and it was sold to the mine. I think they already knew."

"I know the mine, Eddie. That's a long bow to draw."

"It's the only explanation."

"Did your mother say anything about it?" I asked.

"No, not to me."

"Sorry, I can't take your case. It wouldn't be right. I'd give you no return, and you'd be out of pocket a lot of money."

I disconnected the call and put the mobile back into my pocket. It would be less than forty-eight hours later before I would be feeling different.

CHAPTER TWENTY

The motel was reasonably quiet. The few guests who had stayed the night were gone, and the Fletchers were still cleaning the vacated rooms. They gave me a wave as I approached the room that was occupied by Grace Holland.

I knocked on the motel door but got no answer. Trying again, this time I was greeted by the buzz of a cicada. I stood there and waited, the heat enveloping me in its wicked embrace.

Knocking the third time achieved virtually the same result.

Looking at my watch, I decided to go and see Nicole. On my way out, I made a detour to see Jarred Fletcher and his wife. "You haven't seen Grace, have you?"

"If her hire car isn't there, then I guess she's gone out," Jarred said.

"Hire car?"

Alice nodded. "Yes. I think she got it from Bonner."

She was wearing a small sticking plaster. "Been in the wars?"

Touching her head, Alice smiled. "One of the perks of being a motel owner. Too many low shelves."

"You should be more careful, my mother always said."

She nodded. "Yours too?"

"Thanks for the information. You wouldn't happen to know where she went?"

"No idea," Jarred said.

"I think she said something about going to the lake yesterday. Maybe that's where she went. Clear her head," Alice said.

"I'll have a look. Thanks."

So I went home. I was willing to help Grace, but she had to be willing to do things my way. And disappearing wasn't my way.

Dolores was home making a milkshake when I got there. Ice cream, milk, and strawberry topping sat on the counter, and she was already whizzing it. "You want one, Mark?"

There was a slight catch in her voice. I looked at my watch. She was an hour early. She gave me a guilty look when I stared at her. I said, "What have you done?"

And she burst into tears.

Okay, not what I was expecting, so I did the only thing I could at that time and took her in my arms and held her close. Her tears made my shirt wet as we stood that way for a few minutes, her crying, me stroking her hair. I kind of felt uncomfortable, but I was the only one there, and she obviously needed it.

"You going to tell me what happened, kiddo?"

She looked up at me with red-rimmed eyes. "Nicole is going to kill me."

A little over dramatic. "Why would she do that?"

"Because I got suspended for a week."

Okay, a distinct possibility. "What did they suspend you for, Dolores?"

"I hit a boy."

Yep, might as well get the shovel out now and start digging the hole. "Why?"

She put her head back on my chest. "Because he deserved it and I got angry."

"If I'm going to help you, you'd better fill me in," I said to her, putting my hands on her shoulders and holding her out at arm's length so I could see her properly.

"He was picking on—"

"Who was?"

"Jake Kendrick."

No, no, no. "Who are his parents?"

"I don't know."

"Okay, sweetie, tell me what happened."

"He's always picking on people who he considers weaker than him," Dolores explained. "He's a bully, Mark."

"I know the type."

Tears came to her eyes again. "There is this one boy at school, Gary Jenkins. He picks on him all the time. Just because he's kind and sweet, and—"

Dolores stopped and gave me a worried look. I smiled at her. It was a caring smile, not my shit-eating got you grin. "I get it, kiddo. He's nice."

"Well, today it was too much, and I hit him and—"

She started crying again.

"What happened, Dolores?"

"I split his lip and knocked him down."

"Why didn't they call Nicole, Dolores?"

"They tried, but she wasn't answering."

I nodded. "Okay. I better get over to the station. Break the news to her."

"I'd better pack."

"Who is packing?" Linda asked as she came through the door.

I looked over at her. "Dolores will fill you in."

I gave Dolores a hug and said, "I'll fix it."

"Fix what?"

But I was leaving.

"Mark? Fix what?"

CHAPTER TWENTY-ONE

It was too late. I arrived at the station just after Nicole had gotten off the phone with the school principal. She looked at me and said, "I have to go home."

"Wait, Nicole," I said to her. "Can we talk in your office?"

"No—" She stared at me. "You know."

I nodded.

She turned and walked back into her office. I glanced at Suzie, who held up crossed fingers. I closed the door as I went in, and Nicole turned on me. "What the fuck was she thinking?"

This was what she needed. To get all her anger out before she talked to Dolores, and I didn't mind being the buffer. "She was sticking up for another kid, Nicole."

"She can't use bloody violence to do it." There was exasperation in her voice. "I'm a police sergeant. How do you think this looks?"

"Did they tell you who the kid was?"

Nicole threw her arms into the air. "No, it doesn't matter. She could face criminal charges for this."

"It was Jake Kendrick," I told her.

She gave me a double blink. "What?"

"Turns out he's just like his older brother."

"Oh god, what am I—"

"Take a breath," I told her. "We'll work it out. Right now, Dolores is at home buying plane tickets online so she can leave the country."

Nicole glared at me. "Not funny, Mark."

Shaking my head, I said, "I wasn't being funny, Nicole. Yelling at the kid isn't going to do you any good. She knows she stuffed up, and she's sorry. Plus, she likes the kid he was picking on."

"No excuse, just because he's her friend—"

I shook my head. "No, she really likes him."

Nicole stared at me. "Oh, no. That's worse. What if Linda wants to take her back with her?"

I knew Nicole loved the kid, but this was another level of care. She was afraid her sister would take her away from us. I said, "Just talk to her, Nicole."

"I bloody well intend to," she snapped at me, although her anger was abating some.

"You know what I mean."

She nodded. "Fine."

I kissed her and turned to leave. "Thanks, Mark."

"What for?"

"For being her dad." Her voice was soft, tentative.

"I'm not her dad."

"You've been more of a father to her than you realize. I knew you were a good person. You'll be a great father."

Not returning home, I decided to leave it for the women in my life. Instead, I went back to the motel and found that Grace Holland still wasn't there. The only ones were Jarred, Alice, and the guy Jarred had been talking to on my first visit.

I remembered that Alice had said that Grace had hired a car. So I went over to Bonner's garage. He was sitting in his air-conditioned office, talking on the phone when I entered. He finished the conversation and stared at me with displeasure. "What the hell do you want now?"

"Grace Holland."

"What about her?" he asked.

I said, "She hired a car from you."

"What if she did?" Bonner grouched.

"Did she happen to say where she was going?"

"No."

"Nothing at all?" I asked.

"Not that I can remember. Is she in some kind of trouble?"

"No, I'm sure she's fine. What kind of car?"

"Ford Focus," Bonner replied.

"Color?"

"Blue."

"Thanks, Rod."

My next stop was the pub. Giselle wasn't on, and I was served by one of the casual backpackers who often stopped on their way through, working to earn a little extra cash. I grabbed a beer, found a table, and sat down to drink it. I was happily enjoying my own company when Larry came in. He saw me, gave a nod, and then went to the bar.

He stood beneath the bell that hung above the long counter. It was a ship's bell, which had somehow found its way to Hopetown during World War II. However, it was a trap. If you rang the bell, you had to buy the bar a round. It was a temptation that some patrons, when drunk, could never resist.

Above me, a ceiling fan spun lazily. Not fast enough to cool the pub but just enough to stir the air. I took another sip of beer and decided it should be my last. It was cold and tasted too good.

Larry grabbed his beer and came my way. "Mind if I sit?"

Pointing at the chair opposite, I said, "No, be my guest."

The newspaperman sat and took a pull of his beer before wiping the foam from his top lip. "I found something after you left."

"What?"

"After Les Jones was killed, the property was sold to Ike Smith, Les's best mate."

"Okay."

"He was the one who sold it to the mine company?"

"The whole lot?"

"Yes. They also bought part of the old Kendrick's place."

"From Henry Kendrick?"

"No, Barry. Barry the Bastard, I was told he was known as. Hard man, roots tracing back to the early days. Henry is just as hard, so I was told."

"Why only part?"

"The deposit only went under part, I presume."

"The deal was worth millions. Enough to buy up other properties and for Barry to become the biggest landholder in the district. They own half the damn local government authority."

"What are you saying, Larry?" I asked as I took a sip of my beer.

He leaned closer as though what he was about to say might be overheard. "I'm saying it sounds suspicious."

"Your conspiracy theory brain working again," I said.

He gave me a wry smile. "It would make a great story. Just think about it. Local man kills best friend to get his land."

"What about the copper?"

"He had to have known it was there," Larry said.

"Yeah." Then I started thinking. "What else do you know about the Kendrick family?"

"Not much. They keep to themselves a bit. They come to town for the local show. Enter animals in the judging. If they don't win it, Ike Smith does."

"You ever hear anything bad about the son?"

"Which one?"

"Either of them?"

He looked thoughtfully at the wall behind me and then said, "About twelve months back, I heard a rumor that Tyrone beat the crap out of a local young man. His parents paid the young bloke a stack of money to keep it quiet."

The paying of money to keep mouths closed was becoming a pattern. "How much money?"

"Fifty grand."

"Must've done some damage."

Larry nodded as he picked up his beer. "Bad temper."

"Got a name?"

"Alan Fisher. He's a plumber. You going to tell me why?"

I held up my beer. "No."

I drank some more of my beer and watched people come and go as I thought things through. A shout at the pool table brought a round of high fives. Larry said, "You all right?"

"Just thinking, Larry, just thinking."

Larry took another sip of his drink.

My mind drifted back to Rendado. "I went and saw the doctor. Do you know he keeps bloody snakes?"

Larry grinned. "I forgot to warn you about that."

"Scary as shit. When I got there, he was milking a fourteen-footer."

The newspaperman chuckled at my expense. "Little exaggeration, Mark?"

"Christ. Not from where I was looking."

The chuckle turned into a laugh. "What did he have to say?"

"Nothing to make me want to investigate the case any further. If I did, I'd just be screwing the client."

"So what now for the super sleuth?"

"I was looking into something else, but it looks like that's fallen through too."

"Then have another beer."

I thought about my earlier decision. "Maybe I will."

CHAPTER TWENTY-TWO

Arriving home before dinner that evening, I found Nicole and Dolores talking in the living room, sitting on the sofa. The atmosphere seemed calm, so I smiled at them both and headed toward the kitchen. I had not quite made it before Dolores sprang from her seat and hurried toward me. Without any words, she wrapped her arms around me and pressed her cheek against my chest.

I looked over at Nicole, who gave me a smile. "Is everything okay?"

"It's fine," she replied.

"Great."

Dolores let me go and looked up at me. Then she stood on tiptoe and kissed my cheek. "Thank you."

"It's all good, kiddo. Just don't make a habit of it."

"I won't. Nicole said I need to apologize to the boy I hit."

"I wouldn't—" I looked at Nicole again, who had a scowl on her face. "That's probably a good idea. Would you like me to come with you?"

In the background, I could see Nicole shaking her

head vigorously. Dolores said, "It's okay. Nicole said she'd come with me."

"Mark, do you have a minute?" I turned and saw Linda standing in the hall doorway. "My room."

It was actually my room, but what the hell. I looked at Nicole and winked at her. "I'll be quick."

"Don't I know it."

Once we were in the room, she took on an even more serious expression. "The magistrate who the Kendricks had hear their case was investigated at one time secretly for corruption."

"Fantastic."

She nodded. "But that isn't all. One of the investigators disappeared. He was later found out in the bush, dead. His death was ruled a suicide."

"What was the corruption investigation about?" I asked.

"My guy is looking into it."

I said, "You need to leave it alone. Call your investigator off."

Linda stared at me. "Are you sure?"

"Well, for starters, the woman has disappeared, and the young bloke Dolores assaulted at school was his brother."

"I know that." Linda paused. "Thank you for what you did for her."

"She's a good kid, Linda. I'm kind of used to having her around. I just hope my kid is half as good as she is."

She pursed her lips and nodded. "I know, but put us in the same room for too long, and we're too alike."

"Hang in there. She'll come around."

"I didn't react when she told me. I didn't want to upset her and left it up to Nicole."

"That was why I went and saw Nicole first. I wanted her to vent at me before she talked to Dolores."

Linda surprised me then. She put her arms around me and squeezed. "Maybe I was wrong about you, Mark," she whispered in my ear.

"Don't get too carried away," I warned her. "Dolores is good here."

"I can see that."

I said, "Nicole isn't even a mum yet, and she's already a good one."

Linda gave me a confused look. "Don't worry," I said.

She asked, "So you're going to leave it?"

"I'll ask a couple of questions, but for now, I'm going to the rodeo tomorrow night."

Linda screwed her face up. "Ghastly and barbaric."

"There might be a few cowgirls there."

She gave me a cheeky grin. "Maybe I could be persuaded to go."

"See, I knew you wanted to."

She reached out and touched my arm. "Just be careful."

"And you care."

We returned to the living room, and Dolores moved so I could be next to Nicole and my unborn angel. I said, "Have a good day?"

"It was okay. And the best part is, I feel good tonight." She leaned over and kissed my cheek. "How about you?"

"I learned some things. Has Grace Holland surfaced?"

"Haven't seen her," Nicole replied.

"Yeah, me neither."

"Are you worried about her?"

"Maybe a little." Nicole gasped, grinning at me. "What is it?"

She said, "Your acrobat is moving around."

I placed a hand on her belly, but could feel nothing. Nicole snuggled in close. "You know what? I hope it is a girl."

"Me too," I replied. "And I hope she turns out like you."

Nicole kissed me again. "Aren't you sweet?"

CHAPTER TWENTY-THREE

Day 5, Friday

We had an early morning storm the following day. Thunder rolled across the plains, a low growl in the distance as the worst of it slid north of the town. The rain still fell, heavy enough to add water to low water tanks. There were puddles on the ground, and a coolness under the gray clouds it left behind. They would clear later, and the heat would be back, along with the flies. Did I tell you I hated flies?

Within days, new growth would appear, ready to fight against the next round of heat and dryness. And the suffocating weeds. But for now, it was enough to keep humans and animals happy.

Seeing as Dolores was suspended, I asked her over breakfast if she wanted to come with me to see the other side of how an investigation works. She looked at me and said, "I can't."

"Why not?" I asked, spreading my toast.

She looked at Nicole, then said, "I have to do some things for her around here."

The other side of home incarceration. I nodded knowingly. "Fair enough."

The Vegemite on my toast was thick. Like some things, you either liked it or loathed it, and with hot buttered toast, there was nothing like it. I took a bite and said to Nicole, "We all going to the rodeo tonight?"

Once more, it was only Dolores who responded. "Some of you are."

I looked across the table at Nicole, who, for some reason, seemed a touch icy since the day before. Even though she had been speaking to me, there was something bothering her. My stare lingered. She must have felt my gaze and looked up. "What?"

I got up out of my chair. "A word."

We went down to our room—the one she was sharing with Linda—and I said, "What is the problem?"

As soon as her eyes narrowed, I knew it was me. I prepared myself for the wrath of the soon-to-be mother. "What did you mean by your comment yesterday?"

So far, so good. My mind flicked back through the many words I had spoken the day before until I reached the comment in question. I shrugged. "Nothing."

Not the answer Nicole was hoping for. She snorted like a bull about to charge, and her mouth opened to give me both barrels of a verbal shotgun. My hand came up and fell across the open hole in her head before she could fire. "All right, I'll tell you."

She took my hand away and said, "You'd better."

I placed my hand on her burgeoning belly. "I was thinking that for young Edwina here, maybe we should get married."

Nicole gave me an exasperated look. Her mouth opened and closed as though pretending to be a Murray cod lying on a riverbank, gasping for air. Eventually, she got something out. "For crying out loud, you'll say anything if you think it will get you out of the shit."

I just stared at her. Nothing passed my lips. I just let my eyes do the talking.

She stared at me.

My stare continued.

She said, "You're serious?"

"About you and the baby? Sure."

She stared at me some more, trying to pierce the passive façade I had brought down. I could see the tears in her eyes start to well. Love? Maybe. Hormones? Most definitely.

"Mark?"

"What?"

"I—don't make me ask."

"Ask what?"

"You know."

I stared at her once more.

"Mark."

The torture was there on her face. "I think we should get married."

And then she melted into my arms and burst into tears.

CHAPTER TWENTY-FOUR

I was late leaving home that morning. Three crying women will do that to you. Two were from happiness. The third, I couldn't tell if it was like the others or from the devastation of the knowledge that she was going to have me in her family. But I wrestled myself free from the blubbering chaos so I could start my way through the humidity-shattered day. I'd start by checking at the motel. If Grace wasn't there, I'd head out to the lake and see if I could find her there. The more I thought about her, the worse I began to worry. She was there—

My thoughts were interrupted by a tap on my Monaro window. I looked up and saw Nicole's red eyes staring back at me. The window came down, and she said, "Are you okay?"

"Sure, I was just planning what to do today in my head."

"Oh?"

"I was thinking I might look for Grace again."

"Okay. What about the Jones thing?"

"I'm not taking it," I informed her. "I had a chat with

Doc Rendado and looked at a few things and decided I didn't want to rip him off."

Nicole kissed my cheek. "You're so kind."

"Speaking of kind," I said. "What about letting Dolores go to the rodeo tonight? Surely you can find another way to punish her. Have her wash the police cars, lock her in a cell, Port Arthur maybe?"

Nicole laughed. I liked it when she did that. It made her brown eyes sparkle and showed her even white teeth. And that was just a couple of the things I loved about her.

"Okay, Jim Rockford, I think I can work something out."

"What about letting her come to work with me?"

"Don't push it."

Once again, Grace wasn't at the motel, so I decided to go out to the lake. Lake Wintaburra was just over ten kilometers outside of town. As I set off, I passed a familiar white 4x4 coming the other way. I braked hard and spun the wheel, and the Monaro brought its square nose around like a bloodhound following a trail. I sped up and pulled in beside Tyrone Kendrick outside of the local Star Mart.

He'd stepped up onto the footpath under the awning by the time I'd caught up with him. He was wearing work clothes. Shirt, jeans, an Akubra hat, and Hard Yakka boots. He looked at me and stopped cold. "What do you want?"

"Have you seen Grace?" I asked him.

He shook his head. "No. Don't want to see the crazy cow either."

"You sure?" I asked him. "She seems to have disappeared."

"Good, maybe she's playing wombat and gone down a bloody hole."

He turned and walked into the shop. I watched him go and hoped that someday soon some Chinese space junk might fall out of the sky and brain him.

I turned off the main road ten kilometers out of town onto a gravel road that made the car vibrate so much that the windows threatened to fall out. Behind me, a large plume of gray dust rose into the sky and hung there like an early morning fog.

Ahead of me, the lake came into sight. Low, but not dry. Not like the river. It was home to a lot of native birdlife, and once a year, birdwatchers from across the state gathered to watch and learn.

When I arrived, there was another vehicle in the parking lot. A smile came to my face as I pulled up beside it. My window came down, and I stared at the face looking back at me. "Hi, Mayor."

Hal Warner's face paled as though he'd seen a ghost. Moments later, the reason was apparent. Tracey's head appeared above the door sill from where she'd been bobbing for apples in the mayor's lap.

"Sorry to interrupt," I said to him. "I can see you're busy with dictation. I just wanted to know if you've seen a blue Ford Focus in your travels?"

"I...ah...I-I—no, no, I haven't," he stammered.

"How about you, Tracey?" I asked with a smile before adding, "You get around a bit."

"A blue Ford Focus?"

"Yes."

"No, I can't say I have. Mind you, I haven't exactly been looking."

"How's the wife, Mayor?"

He glared at me. Jocelyn Warner ran a small clothing boutique in the main street. It was open for three days of the week. The other times, she spent at home torturing her husband. Still, she didn't deserve the way he treated her.

I nodded. Then, a thought came to my mind. "Hal, you've been around for a while. Do you remember the death of Les Jones?"

Suddenly, the man looked like a sheet soaked in bleach. "I...I was around, but it was a long time ago."

He was obviously hiding something, but I let it go. Tracey's head had disappeared, and he was otherwise occupied. "Okay, I just thought you might have remembered something, seeing you were the same age and all."

"Not exactly, I was a few years younger."

"Fair enough. Anyway, enjoy your...whatever it is."

Starting the Monaro, I reversed back onto the road. Turning the gurgling beast back toward town, I retraced my route, wondering why Warner had lied to me.

CHAPTER TWENTY-FIVE

I concluded that Grace Holland had shot through, and since I wasn't working the Eddie Jones case, I was at a loose end. So I decided to surprise Nicole and shop for the baby. I mean, what could go wrong? I'd go to the local clothing store and find something nice. Then I remembered that I'd asked Nicole to marry me. I needed a ring.

Mission accepted.

There was one jewelry store in town. The name on the hand-painted sign said "Tranter's Jewelers." And as with some cases in smaller towns, it had a dual purpose. The second business sold camping and fishing supplies.

When I entered, I was greeted by a middle-aged woman wearing a pink blouse and a white skirt. To top it off, the red lipstick she wore appeared to have been applied by a two-year-old. She smiled at me, and I looked around for a Ping-Pong ball to put in her mouth. "Hello, Mr. Hayes. What can I help you with today?"

I hesitated. Maybe I should come back later. Once the cat was out of the bag, the bush telegraph would have it all over town before I even left the joint.

"Mr. Hayes?"

"What have you got in the way of...um..."

"Watches?" the sales lady asked helpfully.

Yes. "No."

"Cuff links?"

"No."

"Pocket watch? We have a few nice ones in stock."

"No."

"I'm afraid you'll have to give me a hint," she said. "Or we could be here all day."

I nodded. "All right...ah..."

"Laurel," she said, helping me out of the all-consuming hole my mouth was digging like a busy excavator. "Laurel Tranter."

"Yes, Laurel. I'm wanting to buy a ring."

She stared at me. "What kind of ring exactly?"

"One for Nicole...Sergeant Berger."

"Oh, an engagement ring," she said, clapping her hands with excitement.

I could see it now, word ripping through Hopetown like a grassfire out on the plain with a forty-knot wind pushing it. "No, no. Not an engagement ring. An appreciation ring."

"Follow me," she said with a knowing smile.

Laurel took me straight to the diamond rings she had in a special cabinet. "There. Do you know what size?"

I looked down at my hands and tried to picture them as Nicole's size. I looked at Laurel and said, "What size would you recommend?"

The clown smile turned into one of pity. "I'm afraid it doesn't work like that, Mr. Hayes."

Suddenly, two men walked in, both brandishing shotguns and wearing balaclavas. Laurel let out a cry of alarm and stepped away from the counter.

"Get your hands up," one of them snarled. "This is a stickup."

"Yeah, a stickup," the second gunman growled.

I shook my head. "You have got to be fucking kidding me."

Thief number one pointed the shotgun he held at me and said, "You, back the fuck up."

"Yeah, back up," said his shadow.

The first bandit glanced at the second. "Will you shut up?"

"Sorry."

"Right, fill the bag."

"It's not a bloody bank robbery," I growled at them.

"Shut up!" Robber One snapped, stabbing the shotgun at me.

Laurel remained still. "What...what bag?"

I'd seen enough. I walked over to Bandit One and pulled his balaclava off to reveal a familiar face, complete with a million little red dots where the prickles had been extracted. I said, "You're an idiot."

Tim looked at his brother. "You couldn't keep your bloody mouth shut, could you?"

"I know you," Laurel gasped.

I took the shotgun away from Tim and reached out to Trevor. "Give it over, you goose."

Trevor passed me the shotgun, and I placed them both on the counter. "Laurel, could you ring Nicole, please, while I keep an eye on this pair of imbecilic morons?"

"Ah...yes, sure."

Trevor gave me an innocent look. "You couldn't just let us go, could you?"

Tim stared at him. "Just shut up, dickhead. Don't say another word before I bust you in the mouth."

I'd heard enough. "All right, sit down and shut up."

Trevor removed his balaclava. "I guess this means we're not going to the rodeo tonight."

Nicole and Suzie arrived five minutes later. "I would

not have believed this if I hadn't seen it with my own eyes."

I said, "Believe it. They've outdone themselves this time."

Nicole stood over them. "Of all the stupid, idiotic things to do, this might just be your worst. Why?"

Trevor muttered a few unintelligible words.

"What?"

"To pay the RSPCA fine we were going to get."

"Shut the hell up, Trev," Tim growled.

Nicole looked exasperated. "If I weren't pregnant, I'd bash the hell out of you two in the hope of knocking some sense into those damn heads. Christ. Forget the fine, you morons. You'll be going to prison this time."

"It seemed like a good idea at the time."

Eyes rolled and nostrils flared. I said, "Suzie, you'd better get them out of here before they're shot trying to escape."

She arrested the two dim-witted brothers and took them back to the station. Nicole, on the other hand, turned to me and said, "Lucky you were here."

"Those two are harmless," I replied. "Or stupid enough to be dangerous. If you check the shotguns, I'd say you'll find them not even loaded."

Nicole grunted. "Nothing a bloody brain transplant wouldn't fix."

"Do you still want the ring, Mr. Hayes?" Laurel asked.

Nicole stared at me. Laurel stared at me. My sphincter tightened, and I knew I was done. My spine straightened, and I stared at the mother of my unborn child and said, "What size is your finger?"

CHAPTER TWENTY-SIX

It seemed like everyone from far and wide had turned out for the Hopetown Rodeo. Bronc riders, bull riders, barrel racers, steer ropers. Jeans, cowboy hats, beer, and burgers. It was like a Texas cowboy convention under floodlights. And the miners. Most of them were holding up the on-site bar. It was like the whole town was there.

Except for the local firefighters. A call just before dark had seen them dispatched to attend to a blaze. I knew this because Nicole happened to mention that Suzie and Byron had gone to investigate.

Nicole and I sat in the stands with her sister. Nicole had traded her uniform for a pair of maternity jeans and a cotton shirt. Her hair was tied back in her customary afternoon ponytail, but this evening, the vomitron was behaving itself. Her arm was hooked through mine, and her head was on my shoulder. Every now and then, she would look down at her diamond ring, which winked in the floodlight.

Dolores was off somewhere with her friends, and we hadn't laid eyes on her for about an hour when she suddenly appeared with a young man neither of us recognized.

"Hi," she said, sitting down beside me.

I glanced at her friend. He nodded at me from under a large Akubra. "Who's Wild Bill?" I asked Dolores.

Nicole nudged me with her elbow.

Dolores said, "This is Gary. Gary, that's Nicole, my mum, Linda, and Al Capone there is Mark."

"Hello, Gary," Nicole and Linda chorused.

Nodding, I said, "So this is the young bloke who got Dolores suspended."

The elbow came harder this time. Nicole said, "Don't take any notice of him, Gary. He's not long been hit in the head with a shovel handle."

Dolores glared at me.

I said, "Just pulling your leg, Gary. No harm intended."

"It's okay, sir," he replied. "I'm used to being bullied."

My eyes widened. "Hold on a moment, I—"

His face split into a grin. My type of smartass.

"Oh no," Nicole said.

"What's up?" I asked her. "The barfing band warming up?"

"Your child is deciding to dance on my bladder."

One of the joys of pregnancy. "That's my Melba."

The joke went down quicker than a prostitute trying to earn a quick fifty. Instead, Nicole got to her feet and said, "I'll be right back."

"I'll come with you," Linda said.

The voice on the PA system announced that the saddle bronc riding was about to start. We sat there and watched the first rider come out of the chute on a horse named Possum. From where we sat, however, a possum he wasn't. Or maybe he was. The savage kind. He bucked and twisted and pig-rooted until the young rider came out of that saddle and bit the dust in the center of the arena like a parachutist with a detached canopy. It took all of three seconds.

Wincing, I felt the impact right down to the core of my body. Phantom pains shot to my brain, and my butthole clenched. "Screw that," I said.

"Screw who?" Nicole asked.

I pointed at the horse as it cantered around the ring. "Riding one of those things."

The next rider came out on a horse called Midnight. The same thing happened. After that, a young rider took to the skies via Bucked-Off Airlines courtesy of a horse called Bad Habits. Three more riders and I was beginning to see a pattern. Nicole soon noticed me poised on the edge of my seat. "What is it, Mark?"

I turned to her, wide-eyed, like a drop bear sighting. "I think Les Jones was murdered."

CHAPTER TWENTY-SEVEN

Nicole looked at me, opened her mouth to speak, closed it, and then tried again. This time, words tumbled out. "Did someone spike your Coke while I was gone?"

"No. No, no, no, no. I've been sitting here watching these blokes riding Mr. Ed, and all of them got bucked off. Then I noticed something when they landed."

"What? They all got the stuffing knocked out of them?"

I shook my head. "No, they tucked their heads in. It must be some kind of instinct that they have."

"So?"

"Les Jones had his skull fractured here." I touched Nicole's head where the doctor had touched mine. "Les Jones was a rider. A good one. His first instinct would have been to tuck his head in, and he would have hit here."

I changed the position of my finger. Nicole looked at me. "So now you're a medical examiner?"

"No, but it has me thinking."

Nicole was about to say more when the announcer

came over the PA saying that Tiger Smith was about to ride a horse called Sky Pilot.

A great roar went up around the crowd, and everyone waited in anticipation of seeing one of the best saddle bronc riders in Australia strut his stuff under lights swarming with moths and other insects. There was activity at the chutes, and I saw a rider climb down inside and sit on the animal drawn for him. There were a few bangs, and the rider rocked back and forth. Then the gate man released the mechanism on the gate and pulled it wide as fast as he could.

Sky Pilot was a big strawberry roan. He came out of the gate with an explosion of speed and fury. He bucked and turned and kicked, doing whatever it took to dislodge the rider on his back. But Tiger Smith was stuck to the seat like a joey in a pouch.

Time burned by in what seemed to be slow motion. Probably even slower for the rider as he was whipped back and forth and side to side. Then it became all too much, and Tiger left the horse as it went one way and he the other.

I watched intently as he seemed to float in the air, and then his head tucked in just like the others. He fell hard, and the crowd let out a deflated moan of disappointment. "Did you see that?" I asked Nicole.

"Sure, he fell off," she said dryly.

"No, did you take notice of the way he landed?"

"You're clutching at straws, Mark," she said to me.

I was about to protest and continue the argument when her cell rang. Nicole answered it and listened before saying, "I'll be right there."

The call ended, and I saw the worried expression on her face. "What is it?"

"Suzie and Byron just found Grace Holland's hire car five kilometers north of town. I have to go."

I got to my feet. Nicole stopped and frowned at me. "What are you doing?"

"I'm coming with you," I told her.

"No, this is a police thing."

"Either I come with you, Nicole, or I follow you in my Monaro. Either way, I'll be there."

She sighed resignedly. "Fine, but you stay out of the way, Mark. I mean it."

"You won't hear a word from me."

She explained to Linda what was happening, who gave me a look of concern. "You're going too?"

"Yeah, I want to see it for myself."

"Hey, where are you going?" Dolores asked.

"Work," Nicole told her.

"Now?"

"Sorry, honey, have to go. Your mum is still here."

She looked at me. "You too?"

"Sorry, kiddo, the night callers have rung."

She gave me one of her WTF looks. "Who even fucking says that?"

I hesitated. "Don't let your aunt hear you say that. She'll wash your mouth out with soap."

"Too late," Nicole called back over her shoulder. "We'll talk in the morning. Come on, Jim Rockford."

CHAPTER TWENTY-EIGHT

The night was littered with insects, roadkill, and those animals with suicidal tendencies. Nicole slammed on the brakes again, and I lurched forward against my seatbelt. She muttered words under her breath that were incoherent, but I figured I knew what they were. "Just take it easy. The car isn't going anywhere."

"Don't tell me how to drive, Mark," she snapped in frustration. "I don't tell you how to PI."

"Sorry," I replied.

We drove in silence for the next few minutes before Nicole said, "No, Mark, I'm sorry. I shouldn't have snapped like that."

"It's okay. I get it."

Out on the flat landscape in front of us was what looked to be a bank of bright lights, the road from Hopetown running like an arrow straight for them. Nicole slowed as we got closer and then stopped next to the local fire truck. Police tape had been set up around the scene, and I said, "That's not good."

"No," agreed Nicole.

We climbed out and slipped under the tape. Nicole

hesitated and turned to me, saying, "Don't touch anything."

"Yes, ma'am."

A large patch of ground off to the right of the road was blackened from the fire. At its center was a small car. It might or might not have been the Ford Focus that Grace Holland had hired. If it was, why was it out here?

Suzie came over to us. Nicole asked, "What do we have?"

"We're pretty sure it is a blue Ford Focus. It was reported alight by George Travers on his way into town for the rodeo. By the time we got here, it was pretty much done. All the firies could do was contain it from taking off. Just as well there was no wind, or it would have been catastrophic."

"Anyone inside?" Nicole asked.

"No, not that we could see."

"Any idea how it started?" I asked.

"Someone burned it," Hank Henderson, the fire captain, called over. "I can smell the accelerant."

"Not just petrol from the car, Hank?" Nicole asked.

"Not this time, Nicole. The car was a diesel. Someone definitely set it alight."

"And no body?"

"No, ma'am."

"Is everything safe?" Nicole asked.

"Sure is."

"All right, Suzie, break out the forensics kit and start working the scene."

"Yes, boss."

"Got a torch I can use, Nicole?" I asked.

She gave me one of her classic hard stares. "I don't want you stomping all over my crime scene, Mark," she said firmly.

"I don't plan to," I replied. "I'll walk the perimeter and see if I can find anything of interest."

"If you do, you let me know," she replied.

"Sure."

"There should be a spare torch under the front passenger seat in the Land Cruiser."

"Thanks."

"And grab my coat as well, can you?"

It was the first time since arriving that I felt the chill of the night. I gave a shiver and walked back toward the Land Cruiser. As I did, I heard her asking Larry about some flood-lights. The torch was where she said it was, and the coat was in the back cargo area. I grabbed it and took it to Nicole.

I helped her into it, and she said, "Thank you."

"Welcome."

"Don't forget what I said, Mark. It makes more work for me otherwise."

"I promise."

So I started looking around outside the crime scene perimeter. Sometimes these things just aren't big enough. However, I found nothing.

Returning to the Land Cruiser, I climbed back in and began to contemplate my other case. The one I said I wasn't going to take, but the more I thought about it, I decided there might be something in it. Tomorrow I'd go back and talk to Doc Rendado and pick his brain about the death of Les Jones.

A car pulled up, and I heard the crunch of boots on gravel. Then a voice said, "What's going on, Mark?"

I looked out the open window at Larry Nelson. I said, "You're like a bloodhound, Larry."

"A good journo never sleeps, Mark. We're always on the go."

"Car fire," I told him.

"Any idea whose?"

"No," I lied.

"I see." He was suspicious.

"You don't know of anyone I could speak to about the old Jones property, do you?" I asked.

"I thought you weren't going to do that?"

"I changed my mind."

Larry was now curious. "Why?"

"A bloke fell off a horse."

"Huh?"

"Focus, Larry. Someone I can talk to?"

"You could try Bert Styles," he replied.

"Who is Bert Styles?"

"He—" A sudden fit of coughing burst from his mouth, followed by a bout of dry retching. Eventually, it stopped, and Larry spat on the ground. "Bloody moth."

"You were saying?"

"Bert Styles. He used to be the foreman out there. Ran things while Les wasn't around."

"Where can I find him?"

"The nursing home," Larry said. "He has early-onset dementia. Poor bugger is only sixty."

"I'll go and see him tomorrow if I can. If they'll let me."

"You might get something from him, or bugger all. I guess it depends on how he is on the day."

While we talked, Nicole appeared out of the shadows. She saw Larry and said, "It didn't take you long, Larry."

"Bush telegraph," he replied. "Any idea whose it is?"

"We're not sure yet. It could be local. Could be stolen. I guess we'll know more tomorrow once the VIN is checked, or sooner if someone comes forward." She left out the bit about being deliberately lit.

While we talked, another police car pulled up. Nicole looked over at it. "Great, Paul is here."

"I thought he wasn't working," I said.

"I called him to take over. A girl with a bun in the oven can only stay on her feet for so long."

"Oh dear, I can feel a foot massage coming on when we get home," I said, winking at Larry.

"What a good idea," she said.

"Hey, boss. Sorry I took so long."

"It's fine, Paul. Come with me, and I'll fill you in."

They walked toward the burned wreck and disappeared. Larry asked, "You looking forward to the kid?"

I nodded. "Yeah, I am."

"Get ready for the shockwave, Mark. When mine was born, it was like a size ten earthquake."

"You have kids, Larry?" I asked, surprised to hear it.

"Sure," he replied. "Even had a wife once."

"What happened?"

"Didn't like the job. I was never home, and when I was, she said I'd changed," he explained. "Eventually, we grew apart, and we went our separate ways. I still see my kids once a year."

Nicole came back. "Are you ready to go home, Mark?"

"Yes," I replied. I looked at Larry. "Be seeing you, Larry."

"You too, Mark."

Nicole climbed in, and she turned the 4x4 around, and we headed back to town. "What do you think?" I asked her.

"I don't know yet. There's no one in the vehicle. Someone could have stolen it. Taken it for a joyride and set fire to it."

"Or Tyrone Kendrick could have done something to her," I said.

"It's something we can look into," Nicole replied.

The rest of the drive home was made in silence.

CHAPTER TWENTY-NINE

Day 6, Saturday

The following morning, I went to see Doc Rendado. The day was overcast, but there was no sign of rain. I'd left the house just after breakfast and headed straight to the doctor's place. He was outside sitting on his veranda, enjoying a cup of coffee.

I pulled the Monaro into his drive and cut the engine, dragging my weary body from behind the wheel. It had taken me some time to get to sleep because of my thoughts about the burned-out Ford.

"Back again, Mr. Hayes."

"Yes, Doc. I have a couple of follow-up questions."

"Sure, fire away."

"The death of Les Jones. You're one hundred percent sure it was an accident?"

"Yes, why?"

Touching my head, I said, "And this is where the blow was that killed him?"

"Yes."

"I was at the rodeo last night, and I was watching the

bronc riders. You know, everyone who came off tucked his head into his chest when he was going to land on his head."

The doctor frowned. "What's your point?"

"My point is that Les Jones was a professional bronc rider like the others I saw last night. If he was thrown from his horse, I figure he would have tucked his head into his chest, and the rock would have hit him here." I moved my hand further back on my head. "I mean, I'm not a doctor, but it's just a theory."

"Maybe he was taken by surprise," Rendado said. "I wasn't there, so I wouldn't know."

"That's fine. But do you think it's possible that he didn't die like you said?"

"I couldn't honestly say either way," the old doctor replied. "But in my opinion, it was an accident."

I nodded. "Thanks, Doc."

I turned to leave. He said, "I'm just about to milk Oscar if you want to stick around."

"Pass, Doc," I replied and kept walking toward my car. As I went, I could feel his stare burning into my back.

———

I looked at my watch. My plan was to go and visit Bert Styles, but I figured it was too early. So I went out to where the Ford had been found for a look around. When I arrived, the overcast was beginning to break, and blue from above was making an appearance. Out across the plain, golden rays from the sun reached down like thin shards and pierced the landscape.

When I arrived, all that was left was a burned patch of dead grass. The Monaro chugged to a stop, and the gears crunched as I looked for first. "Fucking shitbox."

I turned it off and climbed out. For the next few

minutes, I wandered around, looking for anything that might help. I walked around in circles until I was twenty meters farther along the road, where I found a tire track along with some boot prints. One of which was scuffed where its owner had gotten out. I didn't think much of it at the time, so I shrugged my shoulders and started back toward the Monaro.

I had almost reached it when I was brought to an abrupt halt, my blood running cold at the sight of a great big mulga snake slithering out of the black burn. He was thick and moved fluidly.

I shivered at the sight of the reptile. It stopped and looked at me, its tongue flickering, tasting the air. I reckon it had picked up on my fear, and the front third came up off the dirt and gravel verge in a threatening gesture.

What was it they say when confronted by a snake? Keep dead still?

Well, I took their advice.

And ran like hell.

I went one way, and the snake, the other.

When I arrived back in town, it was closer to lunchtime. Just the perfect time to visit the nursing home. However, I got waylaid as I was driving along Linford Street. Parked in a driveway was a vehicle with Fisher Plumbing on the side.

I pulled up in the gutter and climbed out, squeezing between the gate and the plumber's 4x4. I walked up to the front door and rang the doorbell. It was the all too familiar ding-dong sound that the old bells made.

The door was answered by a middle-aged woman who looked at me and smiled. "Hello, Mark."

"Mrs. Hopkins. Is Alan Fisher here?"

"Yes, he is. I'm having trouble with a couple of leaky taps. New washers."

"Would you mind if I came in and spoke to him?"

"Only if you don't keep him too long. After all, time is money."

She showed me through to where he was in the bathroom. Before leaving, she asked, "Would you like a drink, Mark?"

"No, thanks, Mrs. Hopkins."

Once she was gone, I said, "Working Saturday, good money."

"Not if I want to stay in business," he replied.

"Alan, my name is—"

"I know who you are," he said, not bothering to look up from what he was doing. "What can I help you with?"

"Tyrone Kendrick," I said.

Fisher paused momentarily before saying, "I can't help you."

"Are you sure? I heard you had some trouble with him a while back."

He looked at me, and for the first time, I saw the scar running down his cheek. "I don't think you heard me right, mate."

"He did that, huh?"

Fisher went back to work.

"Listen, this is important. The welfare of a woman could rely on what you tell me."

The plumber sighed. He was losing patience with me. "I was paid money to keep silent."

"I won't tell anyone," I replied. "I've seen some signs of a temper."

"Some?" His expression changed to one of bitterness. "He knocked me down from behind and beat me with a lump of wood. That's how brave he is."

"Why?"

"We were in the pub, and I bumped into him. Spilled his beer. He waited half the night until I left, and then he jumped me. But I'm not the only one. He's done it before."

"Why not take it to court?"

"Because his parents know all the right people. I was told that if it went to court, he would get off. Then they offered me money for my silence. I needed some new wheels, and well..."

I guess I understood. "You ever think about getting him back?"

"All the time. But that's not how I operate."

"Okay. Thanks for your time and honesty."

"Has he done it to someone else?" There was concern on his face.

I shrugged. "I hope not."

———

I parked the Monaro in the parking lot and climbed out. Villa Gardens. That's what the sign announced. Home for the aged.

Crossing the gravel lot, I went inside and stopped before a nondescript reception desk. A young lady with red hair looked up at me. "Hello, Mark."

"Roberta. Making extra money, I see."

"I wish." She shifted in her seat and suddenly became all professional. "Can I help you, sir?"

"I'd like to see Bert Styles if I could?" I replied.

"Are you family?"

"Come on, Roberta. You know I'm not family," I said.

Reaching for a clipboard with a form attached, she held it out to me. "In that case, sir, could you fill this out, please?"

"What's this?" I asked, brow furrowed.

"Just something that strange visitors have to sign."

"Are you calling me strange, Roberta?"

"Oh, no, sir, I wouldn't dream of it. That would be unprofessional."

I shook my head. "What is this crap, Roberta? You know who I am."

She leaned closer to me and said, "They're watching me."

"Who is?"

For a moment, I half expected her to say bloody aliens. Instead, she said, "The management who runs this place. So if you could fill it out, please, sir."

I took the clipboard and began putting my details into the blank spaces. Roberta smiled at me and mouthed, "Thanks, Mark."

When I had completed my administrative task, I handed it back to her. "Now, sir, if you'll follow me, I'll take you through to the sunroom."

From the office, Roberta led me along an undercover walkway to another large room. It was open plan and housed a television and a small library of books. She took me over to a man in a wheelchair parked in front of a large, double-glazed window.

"Hello, Bert," she said in her cheerful manner.

The old man looked up at her and grabbed her thigh. "Hello, Iris. Did you bring me some chocolate today?"

Roberta removed his hand. "It's not Iris, Bert. It's Roberta."

He looked disappointed. "Oh."

"Bert, this is Mark Hayes. He's a private investigator."

Bert seemed happy I was there. "Is he going to look at this rash on my balls?"

Roberta gave me an embarrassed smile. "No, Bert,

he's a private investigator, not a *privates* investigator. You know, like Jim Rockford?"

"Pity, this rash is bloody itchy, love."

Roberta said, "It's eczema, Bert. Do you put your cream on it?"

"It gets too hard," he complained.

"The eczema?" Roberta asked.

"No, my one-eyed trouser snake. Can't you do it?"

"No, Bert. The last time one of the nurses did it for you, you grabbed her breast."

This was getting way out of hand. "Oh god."

"Bert, just talk to Mark. I'll be back soon."

"Whatever."

Roberta looked at me and shrugged her shoulders, then gave me a sympathetic look with her big, brown puppy-dog eyes. "Good luck."

Bert looked at me. "What do you want, Matt?"

"It's Mark, Mr. Styles."

"Fine, fine."

"Mr. Styles, I heard that you worked for Les Jones," I said to him.

He shook his head. "No, no. Les is dead."

"Yes, I know. This was thirty years ago."

He said, "I worked for Les thirty years ago. Was foreman on his station."

"Yes, so I heard. What can you tell me about how he died?"

Styles looked at me. "He's dead? I never knew."

I said, "He died while you were working there. He fell from his horse."

"Bullshit, he did."

I stared at him, looking into eyes showing no sign of confusion.

"The man could ride a bloody dust devil if you could

rope it. He never fell off that bronc. I told them. I told them, 'Look for the other rider.'"

I edged forward. "What other rider?"

The rattle of a tea cart drew his attention.

"Bert, what other rider?"

"Nope, I don't ride anymore," he said. I'd lost him again.

"Bert, what rider?"

"Les was a good rider," he said distantly.

I decided to try something different. "Tell me about the copper?"

Styles's head popped up. "Where?"

"Where what?"

"The police. Shit, we'd better get out of here before they find us. My old man will kick my ass if he finds out I stole beer."

"Not police, Bert. The copper they found on Les's place."

"The mine never found it. Les did. Les found it near the Kendricks' boundary."

"What did he do about it?"

"Nothing."

"Did he tell anyone?"

He stared at me. "Don't know."

"Then what happened?" I asked.

"Les died."

"Can you remember anything else, Bert?"

He stared out the window again.

"Bert?"

He sighed. "I'm tired, Jake. Really tired. Can you get Iris to come and take me to bed?"

I nodded and patted him on the shoulder. "Sure, Bert. Sure. Thanks for your help."

CHAPTER THIRTY

I called Eddie Jones, who seemed surprised to hear from me. I said, "Eddie, Mark Hayes. Are you still in town?"

"Sure, yes."

"Meet me at the pub around three this afternoon. I want to talk to you."

"Okay, see you then."

The call disconnected, and I swung by the police station to see how things were going with the car investigation. Nicole was in her office, and Paul let me through to see her. She looked tired and in need of some love. I sat down opposite her and said, "How's my favorite mother-to-be?"

Nicole sighed and threw her pen on the desk. "How do I look?"

"Tired."

"I feel it. What do I owe the visit?"

"No reason. I just came to see how things were progressing with the burnt car?"

Nicole nodded. "I'm getting a detective sent out from Dubbo to investigate it."

"You found something?" I asked with anticipation.

"No, just the fact that the woman has disappeared and there was petrol used to start the fire is enough."

"So you're treating Grace Holland as a missing person now?"

"Let's just say I'm covering bases. How about you?"

"I've had an intriguing morning," I replied, then gave her a rundown on what I'd learned.

"What do you figure he meant about another rider?" Nicole asked. "Could it be the dementia?"

"Maybe, but I guess I'll know more when I talk to Eddie Jones this afternoon. When does your detective arrive?"

"Late this afternoon. I have to organize a room for him at the motel."

"Do you know who he is?"

Nicole hesitated.

"Nicole?"

"Matt Stone."

"Ah, shit."

————

On my third beer, I was still unhappy. As Giselle placed it in front of me, I watched the foam run steadily down the sides. She picked up the money I had on the bar and took it into the cash drawer. When she came back with change, she said, "I've been trying to resist the temptation, Mark, but you've got a longer face on you than a bloody horse. What's up?"

"Matt bloody Stone," I growled.

Giselle raised her eyebrows. "The Matt Stone? Detective Sergeant Matt Stone? That Matt Stone?"

I glanced up at her, and when I spoke, my voice dripped with sarcasm. "No, Giselle, the other one."

"Shit, how does Nicole feel about him coming back so soon?"

My head cocked, and I stared at her out of the corner of my eye. "Shit, you already knew?"

Giselle shrugged slim shoulders. "Small town."

I drank some of my beer. "Bloody Matt Stone."

Now, before I go on, I'll tell you a little about Matt Stone. Let's start with the major item first. He and Nicole had been in a relationship for six years in Sydney before it dissolved. Actually, it melted quicker than an ice cube on main street on a fifty-degree day. He'd been found in their bed by Nicole with a German backpacker who'd been staying at a hostel at Bondi. From all accounts, she was wearing an Akubra and riding him like a stolen bike.

I'd heard about him, but it was only after his transfer to Dubbo and his involvement in a case here in Hopetown recently that we finally met.

"Suave, Fabio, square-jawed motherfucker," I growled in a low voice.

"What's that, Mark?" Giselle asked.

I glanced at her. "Nothing. You know, the last time he was here, he treated me like some incompetent bloody child."

"Really?"

I took a sip of my beer and wiped the foam off my lip. I fingered a rivulet on the side of the glass and said, "Yes, I should have let his bastard tires down."

Giselle rolled her eyes. "Uh-huh. I'm sure that would have done him."

"I thought I'd find you here," a familiar voice said from behind me.

I swiveled on the barstool. Nicole walked over and slipped as best she could between my knees. She pouted. "Poor baby."

"It's not funny, Nicole."

She kissed me on the cheek and looked across the bar at Giselle. "Has he been crying in his beer?"

She pulled a face. "Like a child who just lost their favorite teddy bear. It's pitiful, love."

"Can you get me a soda squash, please? Sad Sack here will pay."

I rested my hand on her butt cheek and said, "It's getting bigger."

"So's your kid."

Giselle placed Nicole's drink on the bar and took money from my neatly stacked coins. I said, "I'm sorry if I got worked up about dickhead."

She smiled at me. "I think it's sweet. You getting all jealous."

"I'm not jealous. I just think he's a knob."

"You and me both," she replied, taking a drink of her squash. She looked at the wall behind the bar. "Be a sweetie and get me a packet of that stuff."

"The jerky?"

"Uh-huh."

"Since when did you start eating jerky? And is it safe for you to eat?" I asked.

"Since now, and probably not," Nicole replied.

I looked along the bar with uncertainty. "Giselle?"

Giselle turned and walked toward us. "Can you get us a packet of jerky, please?"

"Normal, mild, or hot?"

"All three," Nicole replied.

Giselle crossed to the back wall and grabbed a packet of each. "That'll be thirty bucks."

I almost had heart failure. Now more certain than ever that it wasn't a good idea, I reached into my pocket and took out a fifty. As I did so, I said, "You'd better hurry up and have that kid before we end up broke."

Nicole grabbed the jerky and kissed me again. "Yeah, but you love me."

In doing so, she held up her hand, flashing the ring I'd bought her. Immediately, I wanted to be swallowed by the earth. Not from embarrassment, but because as soon as Giselle saw it, her eyes lit up.

"Whoa, what is that? Are you two engaged?"

Nicole nodded vigorously. "We sure are."

"I'm surprised the jungle drums didn't telegraph it the minute it happened," I said with more than a hint of sarcasm.

Suddenly, Giselle's fingers went to her lips, and a piercing whistle silenced the bar.

"Giselle, don't," I pleaded.

"Listen up, everyone," she hollered.

"Giselle..." I glanced at Nicole. "Stop her, damn it."

Nicole kissed me again. "I have to go."

I turned my gaze back to the beaming barmaid, who now commanded everyone's attention. I reached for my wallet as she said, "Mark and Nicole are engaged to be married."

A cheer went around the bar.

"And you know what that means," she continued.

"DRINKS ARE ON MARK!"

CHAPTER THIRTY-ONE

I was broke six times over by the time Eddie Jones arrived at the pub. My shout seemed to go on forever because word had spread like a flood on the flat plains, and people came from everywhere. I kid you not, there was even someone from Harrietville, eighty kilometers away. But the appearance of Eddie Jones was like a gift from a higher power.

"What's happening?" he asked, confused at the ruckus.

Some cow cocky came over and put his arm around me. When he spoke, a hot gust of alcohol breath burst forward. "Great party, Mark."

"It's not a bloody party."

He tapped his nose. "Yeah, right."

The man staggered off to join his friends.

I leaned over the bar. "Giselle, that's it. I have to go. No bloody more."

"It's okay, Mark. I'll put it on your tab."

"What tab?"

"The one I started when this kicked off," she replied.

"But I've been paying for it along the way," I pointed out.

"That was for the beer, love. The tab is for the spirits. I like to keep it separate."

"Bloody hell."

She smiled like the cat about to eat the canary. "Don't worry, love. I'll take care of it."

"I'm sure you will."

Eddie and I went into the dining room and sat down. Franky appeared. "You want some food, Mark?"

"I couldn't afford it, Franky, even if I wanted it," I replied.

"On the house."

"In that case, chips and gravy. Thanks."

She scratched the order down on a pad. "No worries. What about your friend?"

"Same, please," Eddie said.

"That'll be eight-fifty."

Eddie stared at me while I stared at Franky. She shrugged her shoulders. "What?"

I kept staring.

Finally, she relented. "Fine, he can eat for free too."

"Thanks, Franky."

"Just don't tell Giselle."

"Wouldn't dream of it."

She disappeared, and Eddie said, "Why am I here, Mr. Hayes?"

"I've changed my mind. I'm going to look further into your case."

At first, he was surprised, then confused. "Why?"

"Because I've got questions I need answered."

He nodded but said, "I'm afraid you'll have to elaborate."

"The main thing that turned me was the site of your father's death blow. It didn't add up to a horse fall. Not for a seasoned rodeo rider. The second is a report I received about another rider seen out there."

The penny finally dropped. Eddie's expression changed to one of realization. "You talked to Bert Styles."

"I did."

"He always said there was another rider out there. But they dismissed it."

"How would he know that?" I asked.

Eddie said, "Bert was out there with my father checking dams."

"Why didn't you tell me this in the first meeting?"

"What good would it have done? Bert has lost it. He doesn't even know what day it is."

A few minutes later, the chips arrived, drowned in brown liquid. I looked up at Franky and asked, "Do you have any tomato sauce?"

"You've got gravy."

"I want sauce too."

"You are weird," she replied.

"And I'm a customer," I shot back at her.

"Not for much longer if you keep eating stuff like that."

"Sauce, woman," I growled deeply, eliciting a smile.

"I'll be right back."

While she was gone, the door through to the main bar opened, and two large men wearing suits walked through. I'd never seen them before, but my main question was, why the suits? Who the hell wears a suit out here? Apart from Rodney Bonner, but that's a whole other kettle of fish.

They caught me openly staring, and the bigger of the two glared at me. He muttered something to his friend, who also cast his gaze in my direction. Then, picking up a menu each, they began to study them.

I always find it interesting when visitors to a town

rock up wearing expensive suits. It makes me wonder what could possibly bring them here at the ass-end of the known world. It's not a tourist destination. Industry is slow unless you're a miner or a farmer. Drugs? Not really.

They looked at me again, and I picked up my beer and saluted them, then I went back to my chips.

————

There was a gathering on the footpath outside the pub. For a moment, I wondered what the attraction could be. Then I saw it. A brand-new Audi. Eddie Jones stopped beside me. I said, "That yours?"

"Where would I get the money for that?"

"Then it must be—"

"Hello, Mark."

Fuck. Not the two guys in suits. I turned. "Hello, Matt. That your car?"

"Sure is."

"I thought Nicole was picking you up?"

"No, decided to drive." He gave me a big, cheesy grin, showing me perfectly white teeth. I imagined breaking them with a pair of multi-grips, and that made me feel somewhat better. "What do you think?"

"I wouldn't leave it parked there. One of this mob might steal it."

"The car is said to be unstealable," he boasted.

I thought of Tim and Trev. "You've not been around here lately, then?"

He hadn't changed much. A little lighter with the hair, grown a few whiskers, maybe bulked up a bit. But underneath it all, still the same asshole. "Is Nicole down at the police station?"

"I think so."

"Great, I'll go and see her. Until later."

"Yeah, fuck off."

"What was that?"

"I said, must be off."

He shouldered his way through the gathered crowd and climbed into his Audi. After he was gone, the crowd began dispersing, my client with them, and I was left there on my own, wondering how the day could get any worse.

But what would I know?

CHAPTER THIRTY-TWO

"You are shitting me," I growled.

"It's only dinner, Mark," Nicole said for the third time.

I glanced at Linda, who shrugged her shoulders. "I'm with you. I think it's a bad idea."

"See, even your lesbian sister thinks it's a bad idea."

Linda stared at me. "Thanks, Mark."

"It's just dinner. It was either here or the pub," Nicole reasoned.

"Let him eat bloody roadkill for all I care," I snapped. "Stone is a flaming moron."

"You're being unreasonable, Mark. And your jealousy is showing through."

I threw my arms into the air. "Fine. I need to go out."

"Where are you going?"

"To see Ike Smith."

"Why?"

"To see if I can have dinner with them," I threw back at her and slammed the door on the way out.

Climbing once more into the Monaro, I slammed the door like a petulant child. The key started the engine, and my foot went to the floor in a deep-throated protest that shattered the peace of the neighborhood. Then I put it in reverse and stalled it.

How do you stall an automatic, I hear you ask? I did, and that's all you need to know. So I went through the motions again, and this time I backed out onto the street and almost ran into a BMW.

I looked out through my driver's side window into the interior of the stationary vehicle beside me. Two men, familiar faces, were staring back at me. Dark sunglasses, suits, and scowls.

I waved at them, turned, and kept going. However, this would not be our last encounter.

———

The drive to see Ike Smith took me the better part of an hour, most of it over corrugated gravel roads which shook the shit out of the Monaro so hard I swear enough bolts came loose, leaving a trail Hansel and Gretel could have followed.

After eventually finding the main gate to the property, I crossed the cattle grid and spent the next ten minutes following a winding track across flat ground. A lot of things don't make sense to me, and why anyone would have made a driveway like this when a straight one would have sufficed was beyond me. Trees were sparse, and the sheep in the front paddock walked along a narrow dirt path with their heads down as they looked for shade.

Off to my left was a windmill, its blades unmoving, standing sentinel over a dry water trough. Beside it was a shallow dam, almost empty by the look of it.

The track cut back once more, then stretched toward a low hill, more like a long mound really. Cresting it, I stopped. About a kilometer beyond my position, I could see the station house through the shimmering heat haze.

Looking at my watch, I saw it was four o'clock. I guess I was going to miss dinner. I'd wear that one.

My window was down, and the croaking caw of a crow drew my attention. There it was, sitting on the rotting carcass of a dead sheep. Its head bobbed down and came back up with a grisly morsel in its beak.

I let the Monaro start its journey once more, and it rattled down the slope, following the track. Eventually, I pulled into the homestead yard and turned the motor off. I went to open the door and was met by man's best friend doing a hundred as it came around the corner of the barn, snarling and barking.

The blue heeler land shark. A savage beast when your back was turned, even worse when roused to aggravation. Best course of action: wind up the window and stay in the car. Just as it reached the Monaro, it leaped onto the bonnet and stared at me through the windshield. Our eyes locked together in a battle of wills as the four-legged monster tried to decide the best way to get at me.

A loud whistle pierced the afternoon, and the dog turned to look at his master, then jumped down and ran across the yard toward a young man in jeans, a shirt, and an Akubra hat. I immediately recognized Tiger Smith. The dog fell in behind him as he walked bandy-legged toward the car, like he'd been riding forty-four-gallon drums all his life.

I wound down my window. "You all right?" he asked.

"I'm here to see your father," I replied.

"Who are you?"

"Mark Hayes?"

"You the bloke that got the copper up the duff?"

Straight to the point. "Yeah."

"What for?"

"Seemed like the thing to do at the time," I replied.

He shook his head. "No, what do you want to see the old man for?"

I nodded. "Need to ask him a few questions."

Tiger scratched at a scar on his chin. I guess it was a present from a pissed-off horse. "What about?"

"An old friend."

The young bronc rider stared at me and said, "I'll take you inside."

"What about the land shark?" I asked him.

"He won't bite...much."

"Great. I'll remember that as it's trying to eat my balls." Sarcasm is my go-to thing when I'm nervous.

I got out of the Monaro and followed Tiger across to the homestead under the watchful eye of—"What's your dog's name?"

"Jaws."

"Bloody appropriate."

It was your typical station. Homestead, shearers' quarters, machinery shed, barn, shearing shed. I followed him up onto the veranda, all the time being followed by Jaws as he circled, smelling blood in the water. Once we reached the top of the stairs, the dog wandered over to a bed and climbed on.

Tiger turned and said, "Wait here."

So I waited.

Under the watchful eyes of the savage beast.

"What do you want?" a rough voice from the other side of the fly screen door asked.

I squinted, trying to see through one of the many holes that flies and other bugs used as an aerial highway. "Mr. Smith?"

"Yeah, don't bloody wear it out."

"My name is Mark—"

"I know who you are," he said abruptly. "Saw your photo in the paper about busting some dog ring."

I frowned. "In the paper?"

"That's right. Some bloody stupid special edition."

"I never knew."

"Now you do. What do you want?"

"I'd like to ask you a couple of questions about Les Jones, if that is okay?"

He remained silent. Then said, "No, piss off."

He turned away from the doorway and started down the hallway. "I think he was murdered."

The older Smith stopped.

"I think someone killed him," I said.

"Come inside."

CHAPTER THIRTY-THREE

It was a typical homestead kitchen…for the fifties. Rolled edge cupboard doors, others inlaid with fly wire. The sink was a one-bowl affair with the old turn taps and a fixed spout. There were two ovens, the original slow-combustion wood-fired and a newer electric one that was probably thirty years old. The table was laminate-topped, and the chairs chrome-framed with vinyl coverings. It was like stepping back in time.

Ike's wife, Gladys, made me a coffee and set the steaming mug in front of me. "It don't have sugar in it. Ants get into it, so we go without."

"It'll be fine, thank you."

Smith said nothing, just fingered his mug.

"You were out there," I said.

He nodded. "I was part of the search party."

"Who found him?" I asked.

"Henry Kendrick."

I raised my eyebrows. "He was out there too?"

Ike nodded. "Sure, we were all neighbors. Henry was out there, Barry, Brian Warner, Hal. It's what neighbors do. Besides, some of us went to school together before going to work on the land."

"So you were all friends?" I asked.

He shook his head. "I wouldn't go that far. Only Les and me were good friends."

"I heard you were the one who found him."

"I didn't."

"What do you know about the other rider?"

"You've been talking to Bert," he said.

"Yes."

"He always said there was another rider out there," Ike said. "Never found any sign of one."

"The storm could have washed any sign away," I theorized. "It was possible there was another rider."

"Sure, there was also an easier explanation. There wasn't one."

"Did you know about the copper?" I asked.

He took a sip from his cup and nodded. "I did. Les told me about it."

"That was why you bought the place?"

"I never bought it," Ike replied.

I frowned. "I thought it was common knowledge that you bought it. Then sold it for millions to invest in other property."

"Do you think I'd still be here if I'd bought Les's place and then sold it to a mine? It was bought under my name, but that was all," he replied.

"Who bought it if it wasn't you?"

Ike shook his head. "I signed a document to say I would never divulge that information. You want to know, you'll have to find that out for yourself."

The next question was obvious. "Was it Barry Kendrick?"

He just stared at me.

"Were you paid for it?" I asked.

"Yes. The only reason I agreed to do it. I was about to lose this place." He paused before continuing. "Rodeos don't pay much. It's a disease that gets under your skin. The more you ride, the more you want to ride. These days, you can make a living from it. Back then, you couldn't make shit."

"Why didn't the buyer want anyone to know it was them?" I asked.

Ike's hands were balled into fists on the table. His knuckles whitened with the pressure. "I'm done answering your questions."

I stared at him. He was holding something back. "Did you kill your friend, Ike?"

It was like pulling a cork on a fully gassed bottle. He lurched to his feet, his face blood red. A crooked finger was stabbed in my direction, and he opened his mouth to shout at me.

Then Ike Smith staggered and fell to one side, clutching at his chest. "Shit."

He was dead by the time the ambulance arrived. Not much hope for a heart attack victim out in the sticks these days. I'd tried to keep him going, but it was useless. Nicole came after I called her. She walked over to me as I leaned against the guard of my car. "What the bloody hell did you do?"

"Nothing," I whispered harshly. "All I did was ask him if he killed Les."

"Shit, Mark."

Ike's wife was sitting in the back of the ambulance being tended by a paramedic. I said, "How was dinner?"

"I wouldn't know. I got a bloody callout."

"I'm surprised old Matt isn't out here nosing around."

"Don't, Mark."

"Yeah, sorry."

"Did you find out anything?" Nicole asked me.

"I found out that Ike didn't buy Les Jones's station. He was owner in name only. Someone else bought it."

"Any idea who?"

"Barry Kendrick."

"Are you sure?"

"He didn't say as much, but I could tell. I just have to prove it."

Nicole shook her head. "No, Mark, don't even think it."

"It makes sense. The copper was on both properties. Kendrick buys the station and then sells to the mine."

"You need more than a hunch," Nicole pointed out.

"Then I guess I need to keep digging," I told her.

It had just gone dark, and the chill of the night air seemed to get into the skin. Nicole and I were still talking when Tiger appeared.

"You bastard, you killed my old man," he snarled, coming at me. Nicole made to step in front of me to block his path, but I stepped around her to keep her safe. "Just hold up," I said as he kept coming.

He took a wild swing at me. I ducked and went under it. My right fist came up from down near my knees. It hit him hard in the stomach, and he doubled over. While he was bent and gasping for air, I kicked his feet out from beneath him. Tiger hit the hard-packed earth, and I leaned on him with a knee in his back.

"Stop now, mate, before someone gets hurt."

He writhed beneath me, sinews and rock-hard muscle trying to break free. I placed a hand on the back of his head and pressed his forehead down. "Stop moving or I'll bloody hit you again."

"You killed him," he growled through the dust.

"If anything killed him, it was this place," I shot back at him.

Tiger stopped moving and started to cry. I felt uncomfortable watching it and got up. Nicole said, "Are you okay?"

"Yeah. I'm going home if we're done here."

"Paperwork can wait. I'll follow you," she told me.

CHAPTER THIRTY-FOUR

Lying on the sofa staring at the black television screen, there were two things that now worried me. Who'd actually bought the Jones's property, and who was the rider that was talked about? I mean, I knew who the buyer was. I just needed to prove it. But why didn't he want anyone to know?

Nicole appeared after having had a shower. She was wearing track pants and a crop top. Her hair was wet and pulled back in a ponytail. Moving to give her room to sit beside me, I looked up as she grabbed my hand. "Are you coming to bed?"

"Has your sister left?" I asked. "Something happened to her?"

My pregnant significant other smiled.

"Yeah, great joke."

"We could go for it here on the couch," she said.

The others had gone out for ice cream. "Fantastic. You and me going at it like rabbits, and Dolores and Linda arrive home."

Nicole laughed out loud. "That would be funny."

"If you say so."

Instead, we snuggled on the couch.

Ten minutes later, I said, "I need to find out who bought the property after Les died."

"You already said that," Nicole reminded me.

"Yes, but who around here would I see to find out?"

"I don't know, Mark."

"I know someone who will," I replied.

"Who?"

"Rodney Bonner."

There was a knock at the door. I glanced at Nicole. "You expecting someone?"

"No."

I got up, walked to the front door, and opened it. Then I closed it. I walked back to the couch. Nicole looked at me. "Who was it?"

"Stone."

Her mouth flew wide. "You didn't?"

"Just a little bit."

She came to her feet. "Christ, Mark."

I sat down and resumed my study of the black television screen. Their voices reached out across the room as I heard Nicole apologizing for my being an asshole. She looked at me and said, "Would you like a beer, Matt?"

"Sure, why not?" He stared in my direction. "Hey, Mark."

"Stone. Sorry about before. The door slipped."

He nodded. "Happens to the best of us."

Nicole returned with the beer. Just one, I wasn't deserving enough. "What's up, Matt?"

"I've been asking around about the missing woman. You knew she had an order on her?"

"Yes."

"She also had some mental health issues too."

"Yes, I was made aware of that fact."

Stone said to me, "You knew her, Mark. Do you think that she might have done away with herself?"

"Before or after she set the car on fire?" I snapped.

I don't think he appreciated my sarcasm. I know Nicole didn't. "Mark."

I said, "All I'm saying is that her daughter meant the world to her. She had a hire car because she'd crashed her own. There was no way she was going to top herself. All she wanted was to get her little girl back."

"Yes, I heard that."

"Her brake line was cut. Not all the way through. Just partially."

"You know this how?"

"Because I asked questions." My words were short. "You want to find out what happened to Grace Holland? Ask the Kendrick mob. They're the ones who wanted her gone."

"Care to come out there with me tomorrow?" Stone asked me.

"It's Sunday. I'm not sure that's a—" Nicole started.

"I'll go," I said, cutting her off. There was an ulterior motive. "I'm working on something, but it'll be fine."

"Mark?"

"It'll be fine."

"Good, I'll pick you up around nine." He placed the beer on the coffee table. "Thanks for the beer."

Nicole closed the door behind him and turned to face me with a concerned look on her face. "What are you up to?"

My arms slipped around her as far as her belly would allow. "Just trying to help out."

CHAPTER THIRTY-FIVE

Day 7, Sunday

Stone arrived ten minutes early the following morning to pick me up. I met him in the driveway because I didn't want him in my house. Well, Nicole's house. "How are you today?" he asked with a smile.

For a moment, I imagined pulling his chemically whitened teeth out with a pair of pointy-nosed pliers. The image brought me joy, then faded away. "Yeah, not bad."

As we drove, he asked me questions. "What did she tell you about the Kendricks?"

"Just that they used one of their judges to have her committed so their son could get custody of their daughter. Then they put a restraining order on her. I also know that the same judge was investigated for corruption."

"Interesting," Stone murmured. "What was her state of mind like?"

"She was stressed. Worried that someone was going to kill her."

"By someone, you mean Tyrone?" Stone asked.

"Yes," I replied.

"Have you met them?"

"Just their son."

"What was he like?"

"Violent."

"Your opinion?" Stone asked.

"No, I witnessed his anger toward her. I also talked to a guy he bashed a while back, who they paid fifty grand hush money to."

"Did he hit her?"

"Not at the time. If I hadn't been there, then he might have. But yes, when they were together, he beat her."

There was a long silence, and Stone said, "What was this thing you said you were working on?"

"A suspicious death thirty years ago."

"Really?"

"Yes."

"Tell me about it."

I don't know why, but I did. When I was finished, he said, "So you think that these Kendricks people were up to no good?"

"I don't know. But it does seem suspicious."

"Maybe. Sounds like they are your regular outback crime family," he joked.

The rest of the journey was done in silence. Turning off the main road onto the gravel, we continued until we reached the entry gate. Above it, in iron, was the sign "Lionel's Run."

It was five kilometers from the gate to the main house. There were two hands at the homestead. The house was positioned on a low plateau that rose maybe six feet out of the plain. There was a barn and two large machinery sheds. When we pulled up, we were immediately set upon by the yard dogs. Three of them.

Climbing from the vehicle, the first person we

encountered was Tyrone Kendrick. He stalked toward us, holding a large spanner wrench in his right hand. His expression was one of anger, especially when he saw me. He pointed the tool at me and snarled, "What the fuck are you doing here?"

I couldn't help myself. "No point in you having one of them, mate. You've got no nuts to work on."

It had the desired effect as the makeshift weapon rose, and he came at me. Stone stepped in front of him and said, "Hold it."

Tyrone stopped in his tracks, the detective's hand placed firmly on his chest. "Who are you?"

Stone took out his ID. "Detective Matt Stone, Missing Persons. Lower the weapon, sir."

Tyrone lowered the spanner. "What do you want?"

"To talk to you and the other members of your family," Stone said.

"What is he doing here?" Tyrone asked, pointing a greasy finger at me.

"He is my liaison."

Liaison? I'd have taken pain in the ass, but liaison will do.

"What do you want to know?"

"How about we go inside out of the heat?" Stone suggested. "Are your mother and father there?"

"Yeah."

"Fine. You lead the way."

Tyrone turned and started toward the homestead. Stone turned to me and said in a low voice, "Do that again, and I'll liaise you out the bloody door."

As we entered the house through a heavy screen door, we were shown through to the kitchen. The introductions were made, and then we got down to business.

Henry Kendrick was unmistakably the head of the household. He was a big man in his sixties with gray hair and an attitude as big as his bloody station. His wife, Mabel, was the submissive type, but beneath her façade, I figured there was more to her.

"What is this about, Detective?"

"Grace Holland," Stone said.

"What has that crazy bitch gone and done now?"

"She is missing," Stone replied.

"Why am I not surprised?" Kendrick growled. He glanced at his son. "Any idea what has happened to her?"

"No, but her hire car was found on fire outside of town the other night."

Again, the glance at his son. "Too bad. Maybe she lost her marbles again."

"What about you, Tyrone?" I asked. "You know anything?"

"Why would I?" he asked defensively.

"I don't know. Maybe you lost your temper with her, like at the roadhouse? Maybe things got out of hand, you hit her—"

"Fuck you," Tyrone snarled.

"Wouldn't be the first time, would it?"

"Shut your face."

"Enough," Kendrick snarled. "I'll not have wild accusations made in my home without a lawyer present."

I held up both of my hands. "Sorry, I overstepped."

"I am curious, though," Stone said. "It's not like there haven't been accusations of domestic abuse before."

"Unsubstantiated," Kendrick growled.

I glanced at Mabel, who was sitting quietly. However, I could see the simmering tension just below the surface, ready to explode.

"Okay, Mr. Kendrick. There was one other thing. Grace came out here a while ago to see her daughter. Is that correct?"

"Yes."

"And did she?"

"No. We have sole custody of the child, and she has no right to come here and disrupt things," Mabel said.

"What about visitation?" Stone asked.

"The woman is dangerous. The judge placed an AVO on her, and she is not to come within two hundred meters of us."

"Whose idea was it to tell the girl that her mother was dead?" I asked.

"No one told her that," Mabel replied stiffly.

"Not what she told me the other night at the pub," I informed her. "The girl is under the impression that her mother is dead. Quite adamant, in fact."

"News to us," Kendrick said.

"Getting back to Grace being out here...on her way back to town, she had an accident. She ended up in the ER."

"So?"

"It has come to my attention that her brake line was tampered with. Know anything about that?"

"No."

Stone stared at them.

"Is there anything else?" Kendrick asked.

"Did your father know about the copper on Les Jones's station when he bought it?" I asked.

His eyes narrowed. "My father never bought the property. It was Ike Smith."

"Sorry, my mistake. I heard it was your father. Quite convenient though."

"What was?"

"Les Jones dying just as he found copper on his land. I heard he fell from his horse. Not sure that he did. I mean, he was a top rider."

"Can happen to the best of us."

"Sure, it can," I replied. "Eddie Jones isn't so sure. He's certain someone killed his father. So is Bert Styles. Says there was another rider out there the day it happened."

"Bert has lost his marbles," Kendrick said.

"That he has."

"Have you finished now?"

"Sure."

Five minutes later, we were bouncing along the farm track once more. Stone said to me, "There is something off about that family."

"You're telling me."

CHAPTER THIRTY-SIX

Once back in town, I met Nicole for lunch at the small bakery café on the main street. I really disliked her working on weekends, but it came with the job. I settled for a pie and Coke. Nicole, ever the oddball eating machine, ordered a sandwich with pickles, potato chips, carrots, and mustard. Oh, and a strawberry milkshake. Watching her eat the feral concoction caused my stomach to tighten. She took a large mouthful and started chewing like a milk cow. With half a wince, I asked, "Good?"

"Tastes like shit, but yeah, yummy."

I shook my head in bewilderment. She took a long sip of her shake and said, "How did it go this morning out at the Kendricks'?"

"It was interesting. When it was mentioned that Grace was missing, Henry looked at his son. Obviously, it is his first reaction when something bad happens. Then, when they were asked about telling their granddaughter that her mother was dead, they flatly denied it."

"What about the brakes?"

"Nothing."

The third chair at our table slid out, and Linda sat down. "Hey, Mark."

"Linda."

She looked at her sister's plate. "What on earth is that?"

"Have you had lunch?"

"Yes, why?"

"Then don't ask. You don't want to know."

"That bad?"

I nodded. "That and worse."

"Any progress on the missing woman?"

"No."

"You should try this," Nicole said around the mouthful of food she was torturing. "I never knew something so bad could be so good."

"Keep it to yourself, Mrs. Tiger Shark."

She was confused. "What do you mean, babe?"

The tiger shark was known as the ocean's garbage disposal unit. "Google it."

Nicole took a bigger pull of her milkshake and belched. I said, "Man, I can't wait for this baby to be born."

It was then that I noticed the BMW parked outside the bakery. From where I was seated, I could see the two men still in the vehicle. "I'll be right back."

Rising from our table, I walked outside, standing on the footpath under the awning. The motor of the BMW was ticking over. Both men inside were staring at me. The passenger made a gun out of his thumb and forefinger and pointed it at me.

There was no doubt that it was intended as a threat. I stepped forward, and the BMW backed up, out into the path of an oncoming Land Cruiser. Then, as the Cruiser driver blew his horn, the BMW took off along the main street and vanished.

I went back inside. When I sat down, Nicole asked, "What was all that about?"

"No idea."

She stood up, leaned down, and gave me a kiss. "I have to go. See you tonight."

"I'll be there."

Once she was gone, Linda stared at me.

"What?" I asked.

"Who were they, Mark?" she asked.

My face grew serious. "I have no idea, but everything about them screams professionals."

"My thoughts exactly. What are you going to do?"

"What I was hired to do."

Linda looked at me thoughtfully. "Why would professionals be here trying to put the wind up you?"

"Maybe I'm getting close," I said.

"Or maybe this is bigger than a man falling off his horse."

———

Sundays are pretty useless for anything. Unless you're a churchgoer, and I'm not a God botherer of any kind. I could have gone to the pub, but instead, I went fishing. I know what you're going to say. The river is dry. Well yes, it is, so I lie under a large river gum in the shade listening to nature. Never will you ever hear me claim to be a fisherman.

It gave me time to think things through. To regroup. I was now convinced that Les Jones was murdered. Who by was still unclear. I was hedging my bets that it was either one of the Kendricks or Ike Smith. The fact that Barry Kendrick had used Ike Smith to buy the station made me lean that way. Why? Because of the copper. It had to be.

Proving it was going to be difficult.

Maybe it all hinged on the second rider.

My other concern was that Doc Rendado had forged the death certificate. And I was sure that Hal Warner knew more than he was letting on.

The other factor was the appearance in town of the two men in the BMW. That worried me because of Nicole. Although to go after a cop was tantamount to suicide.

That was why they came to me.

I heard the vehicle before I saw it. I was listening to the cicadas in the cool shade when the drone of a motor broke through the deafening chirps. Getting to my feet, I stared out across the flat and saw the BMW coming my way, a plume of dust rising behind it.

Bending down, I picked up the fishing rod. That's right, I took a rod. It wasn't strung or anything. Just a rod with a reel.

The BMW pulled up, and the two occupants emerged. They were wearing jeans and shirts. Gone were the suits. I guess they'd learned the hard way.

I said, "You came out here for nothing. Fish are off the bite today."

They looked at the dry river. Tough guy number one said, "Funny man."

"I've had some practice."

"See if you find this funny, funny man. Leave off the investigation."

"What investigation?"

"You know."

"Mate, I'm currently working two of them. Spell it out so there is no mistake."

He stared at me, his eyes burning holes through my soul. "Stay away from the Jones case. You have no idea what you are doing. The death was an accident."

"And if I don't?"

"Let's just say it won't be good for you."

"Okay, now you understand this." You will note that I didn't think my reply through much at all. "You come near anyone I care about, I will kill you. Besides that, you will have the whole of the New South Wales Police Force come down on you like a ton of bricks."

The bloke who did all the talking spoke again. "You were warned."

Then they left me to my fishing.

————

Linda cooked dinner that night. It was fish—not the ones I caught—and salad. Somewhere between the bench and the table, she managed to put some kind of ranch dressing on it and placed a lemon wedge on the side of the plate.

The four of us sat around the table, ready to tuck in. Nicole had showered after work, and gone was her uniform. I ate the fish and poked at the salad. My inner cow seemed to have left me, and I was loath to eat my greens.

"Is there something wrong with the salad, Mark?" Linda asked me.

"No, it's fine. I'm just waiting for the fish to stop flipping in my stomach."

"Speaking of fish," Dolores said. "Did you go fishing today? I thought I saw you put a fishing rod in the shed."

I glanced at Nicole. She had stopped eating and had a wry smile on her face.

"Fishing?" asked Linda. "Where do you go fishing around here?"

"Yes, Mark, where?" Nicole asked with a sly grin on her dressing-covered face.

A sigh escaped my lips. "If you must know, I go fishing down at the river."

Linda was confused. "But there is no water down at the river."

Dolores giggled.

"That's right," Nicole said. "Mark goes fishing in a dry river."

"What do you catch in a dry river?" Linda asked.

"Sand," Dolores said and burst out laughing.

I glared at her. "Be quiet, you. It's a thinking mechanism. It helps me when I need time out."

"Does it help to dip your toes in the sand, Mark?" Nicole asked before joining Dolores.

"I expect it will after the baby is born, Nicole."

Her eyes went wide in mock horror. "Ooh."

"So was it nice and quiet?" Linda asked.

I nodded. "It was. Right up to the point where two thugs drove up and threatened me."

That stopped their laughter.

Nicole was staring the hardest. "What are you talking about, Mark?"

So I told her about my newfound friends.

"And they openly threatened you?"

"That they did. So you all need to be aware of them."

"I'll have my people keep an eye out," Nicole said.

"Warn them to be careful, Nicole. These are professionals. I'm going to say they've been brought in from the city."

"Who by?"

"That is the million-dollar question."

"Does that mean I can stay home from school?" Dolores asked hopefully.

"You are still on a week's suspension," Nicole reminded her.

"But if I wasn't?"

"Then you would be going to school."

"That reminds me. Is it all right if Gary comes over tomorrow after school?"

"Ask Nicole," I said.

"I was."

Nicole nodded. "That's fine."

Once we were done with dinner, I helped clean up the table, then ran the water to do the dishes. I washed while Dolores dried. Noticing her reticence, I asked, "You okay, kid?"

"I was just thinking about those guys that threatened you," she replied.

"Nothing to worry about," I said. "They're just trying to scare me off the case."

"What if they're serious?" she asked.

"Everything will be fine," I assured her.

Suddenly, Dolores's eyes started to fill with tears. "But what if something happens to you?"

Shit. I had wet hands, and the kid needed a hug. I was becoming too good at this father stuff. She knew what she needed and came in hard, wrapping her arms around me. Meanwhile, my hands dripped soapy water.

Nicole came over. "Is everything okay?"

"Just having a moment," I replied.

"You want me to take over?"

Dolores's grip tightened. "I got this."

A minute or so later, I said, "Are you done?"

"No," came the muffled reply.

"You know my washing-up water is going cold."

"Don't care."

"Do you want to tell me what is going on?" I asked.

"No, you will think I'm stupid," Dolores said.

"No, I won't. The last thing I think you are is stupid," I said to her. "Now, try me."

Dolores stepped back and swiped her eyes with her

sleeve. She sniffed and looked at me with red eyes. "The time we've all been together has been great."

I nodded. "You'll get no argument from me there."

"This is the first time I've had a father figure in my life, and it's really good."

I didn't know what to say.

"I'm scared that I'm going to lose you, Mark."

"You won't lose me, kiddo," I told her. "I'm here for the long haul."

I hugged her again and looked over at Nicole and Linda. Both were smiling at me, but not in a humorous way, but in a loving, understanding kind of way. From Nicole, that was fine. From Linda, that scared the shit out of me.

Later, while Dolores was showering, Linda came over to talk to me. She said, "I *was* wrong about you."

"No, you weren't," I replied. "I don't want to shatter your illusion."

"I think my daughter loves you, Mark. For her, that is a big step."

"He's a lovable guy," Nicole said.

"Don't you two start getting all soppy on me," I growled. "One female is enough. I'll be glad when our son is born."

"I thought you said it was going to be a girl," Nicole said.

"I've changed my mind. The odds need evening up."

They both laughed at me, and then Nicole took her turn to give me a hug.

CHAPTER THIRTY-SEVEN

Day 8, Monday

Monday morning wasn't as hot as the previous day, but I had no doubt that as the day progressed, it would get worse. It was bin day, and I knew that because the wheelie bin outside was overflowing and crawling with maggots. Unlike the city, we don't have a big business waste disposal company going around picking up refuse. Here, we had a private contractor with an open tipper and a hoist that seemed to break down at least once a run.

I wheeled the bin out front and placed it on the nonexistent nature strip. No sooner had I walked away than the birds flocked in to feast on the wrigglers accessible due to the open lid. I was walking toward the gate when a vehicle parked further along the street caught my eye. It was the BMW. These guys weren't going away.

I went back inside and into the bedroom. Nicole was getting dressed. I opened the cupboard that concealed our gun safe. Using the keypad, I punched in the code and stared at the rifles. Selecting the Browning BLR

Lightweight .270 Win with a 4-round mag, I also took out two boxes of Winchester bullets and a couple of spare magazines before locking it back up.

"Mark, what are you doing?" Nicole asked cautiously.

"Insurance," I said grimly.

"Now you've got me worried."

I went out to the kitchen and laid the rifle on the bench. Dolores and Linda stared at me wide-eyed. I opened the box of rounds and started to fill the 4-shot magazine. Nicole watched on. "Mark, talk to me."

"The BMW is parked along the street."

"What are you going to do with the rifle?"

"Show them I can't be pushed around," I replied.

"By shooting them?"

"You're not going to shoot anyone, are you, Mark?" Dolores asked timidly.

I replaced the magazine and started toward the door. "Stay here."

"Jesus Christ, Mark. Don't make me arrest you," Nicole snarled at me. "Because I will."

She shoved her way past me and blocked my exit. "You shoot someone, and you'll go away for a long time, Mark. Is that what you want?"

"It's called protecting my family," I said.

"Let me take care of it," she said. "Please."

I thought for a moment and finally nodded. "Okay."

"Good. Now, put the rifle away."

So I did. While I was doing that, Nicole made a call, and a few minutes later, Suzie and Byron did a drive-by and moved the BMW along.

———

After the early morning issue, I decided to get some more background, and I figured the man to do it was Hal

Warner. I went over to the council offices. It was a large red brick building that looked as though no money had been spent on it since it was constructed. The front windows were aluminum, and it had a set of concrete stairs at the front with a steel pipe up its center for a handrail.

Inside, I found a flustered secretary behind the counter trying to answer phones and do paperwork. I took one look at her and said, "You look like you've had a better day."

"I would be if that stupid cow receptionist hadn't just bloody disappeared," she shot back at me.

"Is the mayor in?" I asked.

"I think so."

"Think?"

"He was the last time I looked."

"Can I go and see him?"

The phone rang again. "Sure. I'll let him know. Greenville Council, this is Jessie."

She indicated for me to follow a narrow hallway, and I walked along the patterned maroon carpet to a wooden door. Reaching for the handle, I paused. The sounds coming from beyond were suspicious, to say the least. Oh well, someone was about to get a surprise.

Turning the handle, I pushed the door wide. The sight before me became immediately etched on my memory, one I could have done without, but shock and awe tactics can sometimes be used to one's benefit when necessary.

Hal Warner's face was beet red. He was standing behind a partially clothed young woman, who I assumed was the missing office admin, going for his life. I hid my nonexistent embarrassment by waving and saying, "Have you got a minute, or is this a bad time?"

Two people I have never seen move so fast. Even dumb and dumber with the rottweiler on their heels hadn't moved this quickly. "What are you doing?" Warner blustered.

His office admin let out a yelp of alarm and scrambled for her missing clothes. "Haven't you heard of knocking?"

"Where is the fun in that?" I asked. "Does Tracey know you're having an affair with someone else, Mayor?"

"Shut up and get out," he snarled, buckling his pants.

"Sorry, I have some questions to ask you."

"Questions?"

I thought for a moment his heart was going to give out, the colors he was turning. "That's right. Questions."

"Good grief, man, couldn't they wait? Couldn't you see I was in the middle of something?"

I nodded. "You were in the middle of something, all right. But I think I saved your life by interrupting. You were an awful color. Much like the one you are now."

The office admin took no time at all to dress and headed for the door. "Kelly, wait."

"Maybe later, Mr. Mayor."

With the woman's departure, I had the mayor's undivided attention and closed the door. Warner sat down. "What do you want, Mr. Hayes?"

"Les Jones."

"Not that again. I told you I know nothing about his death."

"I heard you were friends with Henry Kendrick."

He nodded. "That's right."

"Henry's father, Barry. Bad Barry, isn't that what the locals called him?"

Warner picked up a pen and started fiddling with it. "Some did."

"Not long after Les Jones died, he bought Les's station."

Warner shook his head. "No, that was Ike Smith."

I said, "Are you sure? I heard that Ike bought it out of Kendrick's money. Then it was sold to the mine."

"I don't know who told you that, but they were mistaken. If Barry had bought that place, Henry would have told me."

I looked around the office. There was a big picture of an open-cut mine. "Is that it?"

Warner nodded. "Yes."

"Why would you have a picture of it on your wall, Mayor?" I asked.

"They are a big asset to the town. They donate money to certain things and sponsor sports teams. They sponsor Tiger Smith. And without the mine, there would be no town. The best thing that happened was the discovery of copper. It kept us on the map instead of a decaying ruin."

"That bad, huh?"

"Without a doubt."

"Why do they put so much money into the town?"

"Because they are generous and realize that without their money, we wouldn't be able to do certain things."

I stared at it thoughtfully. "Is the real estate office the same one as it was thirty years ago?"

"It is." He sounded proud of the fact.

"Thanks."

I left without asking any further questions. If he knew anything, he wasn't about to tell me. So I would go to the real estate office and ask there.

CHAPTER THIRTY-EIGHT

Crown Real Estate had a small office proudly stating its establishment date as 1988. After parking the Monaro out front in a pothole that resembled a meteor crater, I went inside. The front office contained two desks and a wall of plastic racks containing listing photos of sale properties. One section was for rentals and held only four options.

A young lady looked up from where she was seated. Her blonde hair was in a bun, and her long-sleeved white cotton blouse was neatly pressed. I imagined that her desk was hiding a dark skirt. The second desk was vacant.

She smiled warmly. "Can I help you?"

I took out my ID. "I'm Mark—"

"I know who you are, Mr. Hayes," she said, cutting me off.

"Then you have me at a disadvantage, Miss…"

"Crown. Holly Crown. My grandfather started this office."

"Really? Fantastic. If you have a little time, I would like to ask you some questions which may help me on a case I'm working."

"Sure, if I can."

"It would date back to the time when this office opened. The sale of a station to a mine. Peak Vale Copper."

"Sure. The mine does a lot for the town, you know. Even if it isn't obvious."

"The mayor said that," I replied. "Did the sale go through this office?"

"I think it did, yes."

"You wouldn't have the records, would you?"

"Might I ask why you need to see them?" Holly asked.

"There is some conjecture about who bought and sold the property. I was told it was Ike Smith."

Her face fell. "Oh, poor man."

"Yes. But I talked to him before he passed, and he told me that he bought it for Barry Kendrick, who then sold it to Peak Vale Copper."

"I'm not sure I should be showing you the documents," Holly said.

I gave her my best award-winning smile, complete with puppy-dog eyes. "I'm trying to rule out the possibility of a murder. I already know the details. I just need to confirm it. It would help me greatly, Holly."

She returned my look with one of her own. "Maybe just a quick look. Follow me."

When she rose from her desk, I saw that I had been so far off base about the skirt. Instead, she had on a pair of white shorts with a pleat in the front.

Opening a door into a back room that reminded me of the newspaper archives, Holly led me through well-organized stacks. I followed her along a row, and she stopped in front of a box. She tapped it and said, "This one."

I lifted it down for her and took the lid off. Conveniently for me, the phone in the office started ringing. Holly looked at me. "Blast. I'll be right back."

I sifted through the paperwork while she was gone, and by some miracle, the document I was after was about halfway through. This was for the sale to Ike Smith. I took it out and perused it quickly. I frowned when I came to the second-to-last page. There were four signatures at the bottom. The Vendor, who I assume was Eddie Jones's mother. The second one was Bass Crown, the third was Ike Smith, and the last was Barry Kendrick. Using my phone, I took a picture of it. Then, I put the document back.

I replaced the box on its shelf and headed back out into the main office. Holly Crown was just finishing her call. "How did you go?"

"Fine. It all looks to be good."

"Great. Was there anything else? I have to go out."

With a shake of my head, I said, "No, that was it."

Scooping her keys off the desk, she said, "Then I shall be off. I have a house to show over at Horace Street."

She gave me a wave through her windscreen as she drove away. I climbed into the Monaro and was about to start the growling beast when I got a call from Nicole.

"Doc Rendado is dead."

———

The ambulance with the body in it was just leaving when I arrived. On site were Nicole, Suzie, and the local snake catcher. Nicole walked over to me and said, "You didn't need to come, Mark."

"What happened?"

"Looks like he was milking one of his snakes, and he got tagged."

I nodded. "He said the other day he was thinking of

getting out. Said he was getting too slow. Where did it get him?"

"On the left hand."

The snake catcher held up a bag. "The culprit is in here."

"What will happen to all his snakes?" I asked.

"I'll take them out in the scrub and let them go," the catcher said. "It was lucky we found this one still in the room."

"Why is that?" I asked.

"Being loose in there for as long as he was, they usually find a way out."

"Well, if it was only this morning, then maybe he didn't have time," I replied.

"It wasn't this morning."

I looked at Nicole. "He's been there since yesterday morning?"

She shook her head. "No, it happened last evening as far as we could tell. As I said, the theory is that he was milking and got tagged."

"Last evening?" I asked.

"That's right."

"But he never milked in the evening," I told her. "Rendado was very specific about that when he told me. He said his reflexes were sharper in the morning."

"Maybe he decided to do one last evening," Nicole said. "I don't know."

"Can I have a look inside?"

"I guess so. I thought you were afraid of snakes."

"Terrified," I replied.

Nicole shook her head. "Knock yourself out."

The room looked much as it had the last time I was in there. The snakes seemed to follow my movements. The cage that the snake had come from was on a table in the center of the room where Rendado worked.

Everything seemed fine.

The catcher came in behind me. "Some fine specimens in here."

"If you say so," I replied. I stared at his shirt. There was a name embroidered on it. "Ken."

"Shame to let all his good work go. I caught a lot of them for the doc."

"Did he ever mention to you about only milking them in the morning?" I asked.

"No, but that was when he used to do it."

"So you think it was odd that he would do one last evening?"

"Maybe, maybe not." The catcher nodded at the case. "The odd part is why he had the case on the table."

"What do you mean?"

"He's got the case on the table where he works. When you're milking a mulga, you don't want nothing in your way. Then there is his snake hook."

I looked around the room. It was leaning against the wall where we'd entered. "Would he use that to help him milk, Ken?"

"Yes. You don't go sticking your hand in a cage to get a snake out."

More questions seemed to be arising all the time. "What would you say happened?"

Ken shrugged. "I don't know, but I would say he wasn't milking a bloody snake."

"Thanks, Ken."

CHAPTER THIRTY-NINE

With questions floating around in my head, I went to my tree of knowledge: Larry at the paper. He took one look at me as I came through the door and said, "Boy oh boy, you have kicked over a rock on this one."

I frowned. "What do you mean?"

"Word is that Geraldine Robinson is coming to town in a few days."

"Who is she?" I asked.

"The president of Peak Vale Copper."

"Why is she coming here?" I asked.

"You, my friend," he replied. "Because of you."

"I didn't do anything."

"You've brought into question the sale of Les Jones's land. If what you are digging around in comes to fruition, you will tarnish the company's reputation, and it could cost them a lot of money."

"That answers a question I have," I muttered.

"What?"

"There are two blokes driving around town in a BMW. Heavies. I'd say they work for the mine. They threatened me out by the river."

"We're talking big money, Mark."

I shrugged. "What's a few million?"

"Try billions."

"I guess I'll ask her out to dinner."

"Why are you here, Mark?"

"Doc Rendado is dead," I told him.

Larry looked surprised. "What? How did I miss that? What happened?"

"Snakebite."

The newspaperman winced. "Bound to happen."

"There are some things that don't add up."

"Such as?" I told him of my thoughts. "So you're thinking foul play?"

"Could be. I don't know."

"What can I do to help?"

I dug out my cell and brought up the picture I'd taken earlier. "Have a look at this. Tell me if something strikes you as odd."

He looked it over and shook his head. "No."

"Who was mayor back in the day when this all changed hands?"

"Brian Warner."

"It scares me that you know that off the top of your head," I replied.

"It's a thing."

"What was he like?"

"By all accounts, the same as his son," Larry said. "That's what I heard. He used to ride anything that moved. If it didn't move, he'd push it."

"So the apple didn't fall far from the tree."

"No, sir."

"Why doesn't his wife leave him?"

"Hal?"

"Yes. She must know what he's like."

"Money."

"Hal?"

"Yes. When the mine opened up, his father was given a heap of shares worth millions."

"Bought?"

"No, given. The same with Kendrick and Crown."

"Then why the hell are they still here?" I asked.

"Your guess is as good as mine."

"Any others?" I asked. "What about Ike Smith and Doc Rendado?"

"I could find—oh, I like the way you're thinking," Larry said. "You figure they were all mixed up in this?"

"Ike Smith was on that contract. Doc Rendado forged the death certificate. Crown sold the land. Kendrick bought it. I just don't know where Brian Warner fits into it."

"Could he be the mystery rider?"

I never thought of that. "He could be, but how do I find that out?"

"That is the million-dollar question."

CHAPTER FORTY

I ate a late lunch at the pub. Just a plate of chips with a little salt and a lot of tomato sauce. The main bar was relatively quiet except for a few locals. Giselle was working the bar with a backpacker. I was about halfway through when she came out from behind her bar with two glasses of Coke. She placed one of them in front of me, hard enough for the condensation on the outside to start down like a waterfall. "Mind if I join you?"

"Go ahead. Just keep an eye out for a pregnant woman. She gets kinda jealous."

"I'll risk it."

"Not too busy today," I said.

"No, maybe later. How's things with you?"

"Going slowly. You know. Missing person, thirty-year-old suspicious death."

"Les Jones?"

"Yes."

"You think he was killed like Eddie says?"

"Eddie is still here?" I asked. I'd almost forgotten all about him.

"Still got his room upstairs. Haven't seen him for a couple of days, but he hasn't checked out."

"Were you around when Brian Warner was mayor?" I asked Giselle.

"Come on, Mark, I'm not that old." She seemed offended by the question. I was about to apologize when she said, "He was just finishing up when I came here."

"What can you tell me about him?"

She shrugged. "Not much. Like a lot of the big station owners. Lots of land and money."

"Hal inherited it all?"

"Sure did. But if you want to know about the Warners, you need to talk to the one person who knows."

"Who is that?"

"Tracey."

I was curious. "How does she know about Brian?"

"She used to service him before he died."

"Tracey?"

"Yeah. Brian only died about five years ago. Tracey hadn't long turned up here and set up her business. If anyone can tell you about the Warners, it's her."

I finished my chips in a hurry and then my Coke. Smiling at Giselle, I said, "Thanks for the chat."

"Anytime."

———

After leaving the pub, I tried Eddie, but got only voicemail. So I kept going to the caravan park.

The park was like most of the town. Dry, grassless, and rugged. In more ways than one.

"Oi, you, what the fuck are you doing?"

I turned to see where the voice had come from and saw a skinny, shirtless man berating a younger teenager.

"Fuck off," the youth snarled back.

"That's it. I'll fucking report you. To management."

The young man thrust his hips forward in a crude gesture before turning and walking away. This was the dark side of Hopetown. The place where people went when they had nowhere else to go.

It was getting late in the afternoon. I'd talk to Tracey and then head home. Maybe have an early shower. I found her van. It was an old Millard. The paint was peeling off it, and it had an enclosed awning. The air conditioner on top of the roof rattled noisily. There was a sign on the door that said, "I'M IN."

Pounding my fist on the door, I waited when I heard her voice call back, "I'm coming."

"God, I hope not," I muttered under my breath.

She opened the door and saw that it was me. "Oh, it's you. Finally need some other relief? I could blow you for free to see if you like it."

She was wearing lacy black pants and a white singlet top that showed her large nipples beneath the fabric. I said, "I'm not here for that."

"Oh? That's what they all say at first."

"Can I come in?"

Tracey turned away. "Sure. Close the door on your way in."

I stepped up into the caravan and closed the door. The air inside was cold. At least the air con was working well. I looked around. The curtains were drawn for privacy, and the bed up the far end was messed up. "Take a seat," she said, pointing at a cushioned bench seat along the wall behind a narrow table.

Tracey sat on the end of her bed while I sat on the seat. My ass had only just touched down when I experienced something hard and uncomfortable. I reached down and grabbed it. When my hand came back up, it was filled with a large black dildo, complete with an enlarged head and veins. Tracey saw it and said, "I was wondering where that was."

She relieved me of it, and I was thinking that my shower might have to be a kerosene bath.

"So if I can't blow you, what is it that you want?"

"What can you tell me about the Warners?"

"Nothing."

"It is my understanding that you conducted...business with Brian Warner before he died."

"If you could call it that. I flogged his wanger, and he shot everywhere."

I'm not sure whether I felt uncomfortable or embarrassed. "Did you ever talk while you were doing that?"

"Not if I could help it. I just wanted to get it done and get out of there."

"Yet you're doing the same for Hal."

"That's different."

"How?"

"He helped me out of a situation not long after I arrived."

"What situation?" I asked.

"I don't want to talk about it," Tracey replied.

"What kind of things did Brian Warner talk about?"

"Money, his station, the mine."

My interest piqued. "What about the mine?"

Tracey said, "How he had a heap of shares and that he'd be stuffed without them."

"Anything else?"

"He said one time that he was responsible for the mine coming to Hopetown. Said it wouldn't have happened if it weren't for him and that the town would have died. It was bullshit. Just him talking crap while I wanked him off."

"What do you think he meant when he said he was responsible?" I asked.

"No idea. Like I said, he was just talking crap."

"Okay."

Tracey stared at me. Her hard visage seemed to soften. "You really should be careful, Mark."

"What do you mean?"

"Just…be careful. Before you get in too deep."

"Get in too deep with what, Tracey? What do you know?"

She shook her head, her hard mask coming back online. "Nothing. I've talked too much already. So if you're not going to fuck me, then get out."

Standing up, I headed to the door. Staring at her for a moment, I shook my head, then opened the door and almost cannoned into Hal Warner. He gave me an alarmed look before gathering himself. "Mark, what are you doing here?"

I looked back at Tracey and saw her shaking her head. There was fear in her eyes. I said, "Thanks for the freebie, Tracey."

Warner raised his eyebrows. "Freebie?"

I smiled at him as I stepped down. "More like a sample. Be seeing you, Mayor."

Warner hurried inside and closed the door. Through the thin exterior, I heard him say, "What was he doing here?"

"Like he said, it was a sample, Hal. Honest. Just to show him what he can get if he becomes a customer."

"Is that all?"

"Yes."

"It better be. You know what will happen if it's not."

This mystery was getting bigger all the time.

CHAPTER FORTY-ONE

"I went and saw Tracey today," I told Nicole over our dinner.

Without missing a beat, she forked some pickles and salad into her mouth and said, "For a sample?"

"She offered me a sample, but I declined."

"Who is Tracey again?" Linda asked.

"Local prostitute," Dolores said.

"Oh."

I smiled.

Linda looked at me. "Why would you go and see a prostitute? And what is a sample?"

Dolores rolled her eyes. "Mum."

Linda stared at her daughter. "What? Och…"

"Don't worry, it was all above board," Nicole said.

"How do you know that?" I asked jokingly.

She stopped eating. "Because I would shoot you if I thought any different."

I looked across the table at Linda. "It's true. She would."

"Did you find out anything?" Nicole asked.

"That she knew Brian Warner," I replied.

"Knew, or *knew*, knew?"

"Serviced knew."

"Gross," Dolores said, taking her plate and standing up. "I'll be on the sofa."

Nicole said, "Did you have to bring it up while we are eating dinner?"

I ate some more of my steak. "She said he used to talk a lot while she was doing the deed."

"Come on, Mark. Save it for later."

"He told her that he was the reason that the mine came to Hopetown and saved it from going under."

"How?" she asked.

"I don't know yet. Then there were the shares."

On cue, my mobile rang. It was Larry. "Mark, are you busy?"

"No, Larry, it's not like you are interrupting my dinner or anything."

"Right, good. The thing with the shares checked out. Doc Rendado had shares, and so did Ike Smith."

"What happened to Ike Smith's?"

"Don't know."

"Okay, thanks, Larry."

I disconnected the call. Nicole was staring at me, waiting for me to continue.

"What shares, Mark?" she finally asked.

"Doc Rendado, Ike Smith, Kendrick, Bass Crown, and Brian Warner, the former mayor, all got shares in the mine worth millions when it was acquired."

"So?"

"So...to me, that sounds a little off."

"It does," Linda said, agreeing with me.

"Explain to me your theory," Nicole said.

"Okay. Doc Rendado ticked off on the death certificate, citing accidental death. Ike Smith buys the station from the Jones widow for Kendrick. Kendrick then sells it to the mine. All of them get shares except for Kendrick, who gets a lot more. Bass Crown oversees the deal, and he gets shares in the mine. The only one not clear at the moment is Warner, who claims he was the one who was responsible for the mine coming and saving the town."

Nicole stared at me. "I know you, Mark. Where does Warner fit in?"

"If I had a theory—"

"Which you do."

"Which I do. Brian Warner is the mystery rider that Bert Styles saw in the storm."

Nicole stared at me. "You need proof for any of it, Mark."

"That's what I don't have." I left out my suspicions about Doc Rendado's death.

"You're not going to let this go, are you?"

"No."

"I'll do what I can to help you, Mark, but I won't risk my job."

"I would never ask you to do that, Nicole."

"I know." There was a moment of silence before she said, "Who wants ice cream and pickles?"

"Good grief."

CHAPTER FORTY-TWO

Day 9, Tuesday

Matt Stone swung by early the next morning to say he was headed back to Dubbo. I wasn't happy about the news. "That's it? You just give up?"

"I'm not giving up, Mark. I've just run down everything I can and gone nowhere. For all I know, she could have just shot through."

"What about the car? Her kid?"

"I'm sorry, Mark. If something comes up, I'll be back, but I've got nothing. I'll stop at the motel and check on the way out of town, and then I'm gone."

"Shit."

"I feel the same way, Mark."

"Then stay, damn it."

"I can't. I have other cases I'm working as well."

I nodded.

"Anyway, I'm out of here. Be seeing you."

Nicole walked him out, and I sat on the sofa, simmering with anger. Dolores appeared, reading my mood with a maturity beyond her years, and silently walked over and sat next to me. She put her head on my shoulder and said nothing. We were still that way when Nicole came back.

I don't know if I've said this before, but that kid is special. I'd be happy if mine ended up half as special as she was.

————

This is the part where I threw all my balls back in the air. While Stone was there, I hadn't needed to worry about Grace Holland. But with his departure, I was back to wrestling with two cases. One of which was considerably advanced, the other a stone wall. I decided I needed to see Bert Styles again.

Pulling up at the care facility, I went inside to find Roberta once more at the reception desk. "Hi, Mark, how's it hanging?"

I frowned at her. "Is that appropriate, Roberta?"

"Don't worry, they're not watching me anymore."

"Okay. I'd like to see Bert Styles again if I could."

Her expression changed. "I'm sorry, Mark. Bert died the day after you saw him. Poor old soul had a heart attack."

I was bummed. But he was now better off. I said, "At least he got one visitor before he died."

"Two, actually."

"Two? Family?"

"Bert didn't have family. Doc Rendado came and saw him the day he died."

"The same day?" I asked.

"Yes."

"Was there an autopsy done, Roberta?"

"No. The doctor who declared him deceased said there was no need."

I nodded. "Thanks."

Turning to leave, I had a thought and stopped. "Where did they take him?"

"I assume he is at the funeral home. I think they are cremating him tomorrow."

"Thanks, Roberta."

Back out in the Monaro, I began wondering about the connections in the deaths of Styles and Rendado. It couldn't be a coincidence. It seemed strange that Rendado had visited Bert the day he died and then died himself.

I needed to see the body. Turning the key on the Monaro, it burbled to life, and I pulled onto the street from the parking lot. My next stop was going to be the funeral home, and I just hoped Frank Ferris was forgiving.

———

When I arrived at the big sleep station, I hesitated before going in. Something told me Ferris wasn't much of a forgiving bloke. Since he was out on bail, things might get a little awkward. After sitting for several minutes, building up my courage, I turned off the motor and climbed out, locking the Monaro and going inside. There were flowers in vases scattered around the reception area. Not real ones. They wouldn't last ten minutes in this climate. Fake. The ones with the bright colors and the glossy leaves. Give them a wipe and they're good to go.

Soft music played in the background, and there were pamphlets on a small table for the public to take. I looked behind the counter and saw that I was in luck. Ferris wasn't there. Instead, it was his missus. She was wearing a black suit and thick makeup. At the corner of her left eye was a teardrop tattoo. I was guessing there were more below the clothes she wore.

She took one look at me and said, "What do you want?"

"Is that any way to talk to a potential customer?" I asked.

"Come back when you're ready to be cooked."

"Look, I know I'm not your favorite person right about now. I get that. But I need your help with something."

"What?"

"I need to see Bert Styles's body."

"Piss off."

"It's important," I replied.

"I don't care," she growled.

"Listen," I shot back at her. "Are you really pissed at me or at your old man, who did something stupid and got caught?"

"Both of you, now go away, or I will call the police and have you arrested for trespass."

I held my hands up, palms outward, in a gesture of concession. "Okay, okay. I'll go. Sorry to have bothered you."

I walked out into the heat and climbed into the Monaro. Staring at the funeral home, I knew what I was going to do. Wait for dark and come back.

CHAPTER FORTY-THREE

Leaving town, I drove out to the Smith property. I had the distinct feeling that I wouldn't be welcome there either, but I needed to talk to Ike's wife. As I bumped into the yard, I was greeted again by the land shark. Jaws seemed to be more subdued on this visit—well, at least a little less ferocious than before. It was, however, the two-legged kind that I needed to be wary of.

This time when he came at me, he was swinging a spanner. "You really don't need to do this again," I told him as he stormed across the yard from the machinery shed.

"Get the fuck off my property," he snarled at me.

"I just want to talk to your mother. That's all."

"So you can bloody kill her too?"

The spanner made a whistling sound as he swung it. There was no holding back. I went under the swing and did the same as last time. He had not learned. My fist hit him in the stomach, and he doubled over. He went down on his knees, gasping for breath. I stood over Tiger and waited for his reaction. He staggered to his feet and let out a roar as he started swinging the spanner again.

Had any of the blows connected, he would have killed me. I have no doubt about that. However, the torturous hours my mother had inflicted upon me in Mrs. Zambosa's ballet class remained with me after all these years. I danced left and right, evading Tiger's wild swings. All the while, I was trying to get him to stop.

"Will you knock it off?" I shouted at him.

"Your head? Sure as shit I will."

"Enough!"

The screech reached out across the yard from the veranda of the main homestead. Tiger looked at his mother and spat in the dirt. "I'm just getting rid of him."

"Go back to your work, Tiger. I'll deal with him."

"But—"

"Go on now. And take the dog with you."

Tiger disappeared into the workshop with the land shark close behind. I stood there gathering myself, waiting for Gladys Smith to invite me inside.

"What do you want?" she asked brusquely.

"I came to talk to you about what Ike told me before he died."

"About him buying the Jones place with Kendrick's money?"

"Yes."

"Come inside."

We went through to the kitchen. It smelled like she'd been cooking, and when I saw her bench laden with scones, my suspicions were confirmed. She said, "I'll make a cup of tea."

"Thank you."

I waited in silence while she prepared the drinks. When she was done, she asked me, "Would you like a scone?"

My insides had been doing cartwheels ever since I'd arrived, hoping she would ask. "No, thank you."

I was being polite, hoping that she would insist, but it didn't come. Sitting down, she asked, "How is the baby coming along?"

"Not fast enough," I replied. "I wish it would get here so I could meet it."

"You should try being pregnant if you think time is going too slow."

There was a drawn-out silence before I said, "Ike got shares from the mining company when they acquired the Smith place."

Gladys nodded slowly. "Yes."

"So did some of the others. Barry Kendrick, Doc Rendado, Brian Warner, and Bass Crown. Millions of dollars' worth."

"I wouldn't know," she lied.

"Come on, Gladys. You can't hurt him now. A man was murdered for his land."

She looked at me strangely. "What?"

"Les Jones. Someone killed him."

"But it was an accident. That was the finding."

"I think it was otherwise. What can you tell me about the shares?"

Gladys nodded. "They were given to Ike because of what he did. We didn't think it was illegal. Barry Kendrick just said that he didn't want anyone to know he was buying it. He offered to help us if we did it."

"How?"

"We were in debt. Ike loved this place, but it was a money pit. So he agreed. Then, Barry came to us a time later and said he was selling it to the mine. Ike didn't like it, but we didn't own it. Barry said it was a way of helping the town. Hopetown was slowly dying, and with the mine coming, there would be a lot more money, and it would breathe new life into the town. When it was all done, we were given quite a few shares."

"What happened to it?" I asked.

Gladys waved her hand in the air. "This place. It chewed through it like a starving dog."

"What are you going to do now?"

"Work it until the bank takes it all," she replied. "Ike wouldn't give up. Neither will I."

"Did you think the whole sale thing was strange?" I asked Gladys.

"It was, but like I said, we needed the money, and the town needed the mine."

"It was that bad?"

"If the copper hadn't been found, then the town would have been lucky to last another two years. Yes, it was that bad."

"When did you find out about the copper?"

Gladys shrugged. "I'm not sure."

"Les told Ike about the copper. Did he tell anyone else?"

"I don't know."

I finished my tea. "I won't keep you anymore. Thank you for the tea."

"I'm sorry about my son. I don't blame you for Ike's death. It was this place that killed him."

I said my goodbyes and climbed into the Monaro. As I drove away, I knew everything revolved around a certain group of people. I still didn't know who'd killed Les Jones, but I think I knew why.

As I bumped over the track from the homestead to the road, my phone rang. I stopped and checked it. The number was blocked. I thought about not answering it, but I did anyway. "Mark Hayes."

"Mr. Hayes, my name is Geraldine Robinson. I'd like to organize a time for us to meet, if that is possible?"

"You from Peak Vale Copper?"

"Yes, I am."

"All right. Where do you want to meet?" I asked.

Geraldine said, "I will be in town tomorrow. Perhaps we could meet for lunch?"

"Are you buying?" I asked her.

"Sure."

"Then it's a date. I'll see you at the pub at twelve."

"I'll look forward to it. Oh, why don't you bring your lovely partner with you? Nicole, isn't it?"

That threw me. "She's very busy."

"What about her sister? Linda? Maybe Dolores? No limit on the budget."

"I'll see you at twelve," I told her and hung up.

CHAPTER FORTY-FOUR

With a bit of time up my sleeve, I went to the motel on the off chance and, by all improbability, that Grace had reappeared. Of course, she hadn't.

I knocked on her room door and got no answer. Turning to leave, I almost walked into Jarred Fletcher. "She still isn't back. After all this time, I'd say she's gone."

"Has her room been cleaned?" I asked.

"No. We were going to give it another couple of days and then go through it. Not that there is any rush."

"Do you mind if I have a look through it?" I asked him.

Jarred shrugged. "The police already went through it and found nothing."

"I'd still like to look, if that's okay?"

"I'll get you a key."

A few minutes later, Jarred returned. He offered me the key and said, "Just drop it to Alice when you're done."

"Sure."

As I opened the room, I was hit in the face by a waft

of stale air. At one time, someone had smoked in the room, and the carpet had soaked it up. The heat of the day acted like a release button.

I looked around the room and found nothing. Stone had obviously turned it over because stuff was scattered everywhere. I sat on the side of the bed, my arms resting on my knees, looking at the manky carpet. I tried to work out scenarios of what could have happened to her.

I leaned down and picked up some flakes from the carpet. They were small pieces of chipboard. I dropped them back on the floor and stood up. There was nothing here. Time to go.

———

Whether it was by chance or some other intervention, I went to the café on Main Street to get a sandwich. Grabbing a ham and cheese on fresh bread and a can of Solo, I paid the exorbitant price for them and was on my way out into the still-rising heat of the day when Tracey came in through the streamer curtain. She was wearing dark sunglasses and a long-sleeved shirt.

"Tracey?"

"Mark," she replied and kept walking.

I sat outside under the awning and waited for her to reappear. I never opened the sandwich because it would have issued an invitation to the swarm of flies who would compete with me for the first bite.

When Tracey emerged a couple of minutes later, I got to my feet. She had been headed in my direction until she saw me, then hurriedly broke off and started the other way. "Tracey, wait."

She kept walking.

"Stop, or I'll call Nicole." It was all I could think of at the time.

It worked because she stopped and turned to face me. I said, "Warner?"

Tracey frowned. "Warner, what?"

"The beating that you got."

"What beating? I don't know what you're talking about."

I said, "Dark sunglasses inside, long sleeves to cover the bruises. You don't ever wear clothes like that."

She grabbed at the collar of her shirt and screwed her hand into a fist.

"Take off the glasses."

There was a moment of hesitation, and then Tracey did as I asked. She had tried to hide the bruising and swelling around her left eye and on her cheek with makeup, but hadn't been successful. Hence the oversized glasses. Her eye was half closed.

"Did Warner do that?" I asked again.

Tracey gave a slow nod.

"Because of me?"

"Yes."

"Why?" I asked.

"Because of you."

I turned to face the street, maybe to seethe or perhaps because I thought he might be somewhere close by. The only thing I saw was the BMW. The boys were still on the job. "Go home and put some ice on that eye, Tracey. Everything will be fine."

As I strode purposefully toward the Monaro, Tracey watched me go. "Mark, what are you going to do?"

"See a man about manners."

"Mark, leave it."

The Monaro bore the brunt of my ire at first. The door slammed when I climbed in, and I revved the guts out of the engine when it started. I shoved it violently into reverse and then peeled rubber when I took off. You could have heard the beast from Dubbo, she was that loud.

The deep roar of the motor was soon joined by the howl of a police siren because at that time, Senior Constable Paul Wills chose to drive in the opposite direction. In the shotgun seat was Suzie.

There was no way I was stopping. I just kept the pedal down, and the beast howled in protest. When I turned out of the main street, the Monaro slid sideways. I corrected the slide and almost slammed my foot through the floor. The car roared again.

When I stopped in the parking lot, the Monaro slid sideways once more. I threw the door open and started toward the entrance. Behind me, the howling of the police siren stopped, and the two officers shouted at me. "Mark, stop!"

I ignored them and went inside. Storming through the reception area, I glanced at the gatekeeper. "Is he in?"

"Mr. Warner is bus—"

By the time she got that far, I was gone.

When I reached the office, the door barred my way. The door handle was just a nuisance to be avoided, and I used my boot to open it. The obstruction flew back with a sharp sound of splintering wood, followed by the crash of the handle putting a hole in the wall.

Warner's head flew up from his work, and terror filled his eyes as I stalked over to the desk. Holding both hands up defensively, he said, "Now, Mark, wait a minute—"

They say violence doesn't solve anything. But, by Christ, sometimes it feels good.

I grabbed a handful of his collar and dragged him halfway across the desk before I hit him the first time. It was followed by another, and blood flowed freely. I managed two more before Paul and Suzie dragged me off him.

"Damn it, Mark. What are you doing?"

"Just give me a minute to finish, will you?" I snarled.

"Mark, no," Suzie shouted at me to break through the curtain of rage.

In this brief period of time, Paul had forced my hands behind my back and placed handcuffs on me. He then shoved me face-first against a wall. The last I saw of Warner was him slumped, bleeding in his chair.

When I hit the wall, a whoosh of air escaped my lungs. Then Paul leaned in close to my ear and said, "I'd hate to be you when the sarge gets here."

Fuck.

CHAPTER FORTY-FIVE

"What the hell were you thinking?" Nicole snarled at me. I was seated on the floor with my back to the wall.

Hal Warner was out in the reception area getting checked over by the ambos. From all reports, he had a broken nose and a split lip.

"Are you going to tell me what happened?" she demanded.

"I lost my temper," I replied.

"Why? This isn't like you, Mark. This violence scares me."

I glanced at Paul, who was staring at me with his arms crossed. "It was lucky there wasn't any more damage done. The strange part is that Warner doesn't want to press charges."

"Neither should he."

"But that doesn't mean we won't," Nicole snapped.

I remained silent.

"Well?"

"He beat the crap out of Tracey after I talked to her."

"That's why he won't press charges," Paul said.

"It doesn't excuse what you did," Nicole snapped. "There are proper channels."

I remained silent.

"By the way, the speeding ticket will stand."

She stared at me.

"Okay, get out of here," Nicole growled. "We'll talk about this some more tonight."

I got to my feet, and on the way out, I had to walk past where Warner was being attended to. I stopped. Suzie noticed.

"Mark, keep walking."

"What are you hiding, Hal?" I asked him. "You and the others. You're all hiding something. What is it?"

Suzie gave me a shove. "Out. Now."

"Careful, Mark," I heard Warner say. "You have more to lose than I do."

I turned and took a step toward him. "What the fuck did you say?"

"Mark!" Suzie snapped. "Get."

"You heard him. He threatened me."

She stepped in front of me. "If I have to, I will arrest you. Go."

With a heaving sigh, I turned and walked out to the Monaro. The door was as I'd left it—open, and inside was like a furnace. When I sat down, I could feel the heat of the seat burning through my jeans. Closing the door, I started the motor. It chugged to life with its deep-throated growl. Then I proceeded to bash the steering wheel with the palm of my hand, berating myself for being so stupid.

———

After leaving the council offices, I went to the newspaper.

Larry took one look at me and said, "Someone pissed in your porridge, huh?"

I told him what had happened with Hal Warner.

"That will ruin your day."

"Tell me about it," I replied. "I have a meeting with Geraldine Robinson tomorrow."

"She's coming here?"

"Yes, what can you tell me about her?" I asked him.

Larry looked thoughtful. "She is the granddaughter of the original Peak Vale Copper president and part-owner. She owns a controlling majority. Word is she's harder than her grandfather ever was."

"Have you seen Eddie Jones around in your travels?"

"No. Wouldn't know him if I fell over him. Why? Has he disappeared on you?"

"In a way."

I was about to say more when my phone rang. "Mark Hayes."

"Mr. Hayes, this is Toni Perrin from the Hopetown Medical Center."

Nurse Gladys. "Yes, Toni, how can I help you?"

"I have a man here who isn't in the best of shape who insists on talking to you and no one else. Even when we were going to call the police, he insisted that we didn't."

"What's his name?"

"Edward Jones."

"What happened to him?" I asked.

"He says he had a fall, but his injuries are consistent with a beating."

I winced. This investigation was starting to go places that I didn't like. "I'll come down."

"That would be great."

"Trouble?" Larry asked after the call disconnected.

I nodded. "Yeah. I'll catch up with you later."

"Try not to beat anyone else," he said to me.

"Before I go, when you were looking about for the shares, did anything else pop?"

"Nothing I thought that was significant."

"Can you dig into their past, see if there is anything that links any of them to Geraldine Robinson's grandfather?"

"Sure. But I'm guessing he would have allocated the shares with the board."

I nodded. "Just be careful."

CHAPTER FORTY-SIX

Nurse Gladys came out into the waiting room to see me when my arrival was announced. There was a concerned look on her face, and when she spoke, I could tell that concern had filtered into her voice.

"How is he?" I asked.

"He isn't good, but insists on leaving," she explained to me. "But he should really stay."

"I'll see what I can do."

"Thank you."

She showed me through to the cubicle where Eddie was. She was right. He was battered and bruised. "Shit, Eddie, what happened to you?"

He smiled weakly. "You should see the other guy."

"What happened?"

He started to throw back the blanket that was over him. "We have to get out of here."

I stopped him. "Stay there, Eddie."

"I can't," he said with a grimace of pain.

"You're going nowhere, mate. Not until they say you can. From the looks of you, here is safer."

"Shit, Mark. You're making progress. You have to be."

I stared at him. His left eye was almost closed. The white around his iris was blood red. There was a cut above his right eye, and both cheeks were bruised, his lips swollen. Then I noticed the dark lines around his wrists. "Why do you say that, Eddie?"

"Because you've got them worried."

"I'm going to take a guess, Eddie. Call it a wild stab in the dark. There were two of them. Big guys. They took you somewhere and tied you up before beating the shit out of you. Am I right?"

The nod was barely perceptible, but it was there.

"When did they take you?"

"Couple of days ago."

"How did you get away?"

"They let me go. They said to tell you to stop."

"When was this?"

"Early this morning."

Right before Geraldine Robinson called me, I thought. She wanted me to see this before I saw her. "Eddie, you stay here. Let them take care of you. Do you understand?"

He nodded. "No police, Mark. Okay?"

When Nicole found out, she'd kill me. "Okay."

"Thanks, Mark."

"I'll check on you sometime tomorrow."

On my way out, I saw Nurse Gladys. "How did you go?"

"He'll stay."

"Thank you, Mr. Hayes."

———

"You in the shit too?" Dolores asked me when I got home. She was sitting on the couch, reading the new *Onyx Storm* by Rebecca Yarros.

"Good book?" I asked her.

She nodded. "Sure. I've been waiting like months for it."

I nodded. She continued, "Nicole came home a while ago and then left. I heard her and Mum talking."

I didn't really want to discuss it. "When are you going back to school?"

"Next week is school holidays. After that." She stared at me. "What happened?"

"I screwed up," I replied.

"I heard her say you hit someone."

"Yeah. Several times."

"What did he do?"

"Hit a lady."

"You want me to talk to Nicole for you?"

I stared at her and smiled. "You're a good kid, Dolores. Don't ever change."

"I know. I guess you're suspended too," she said, flipping a page.

"I'm an adult. I don't get suspended. I get arrested."

Dolores placed the book face down in her lap. "You got arrested?"

"Not for the assault, although I should have. I got done for speeding through town."

"In the Monaro?"

I picked up the doubt in her voice. "You start being cheeky, I'll send you back to Sydney."

"Good luck with that."

"How is your new boyfriend?"

"He's fine."

"You kissed him yet?"

She screwed up her face. "Eww. What kind of question is that?"

"Just want to know if I have to have words with him, that's all."

Dolores's eyes widened as she flew off the couch. "You wouldn't dare."

I smiled at her. The horror of the thought that I would say something was still etched on her face. "Mark, no."

"Of course not. Don't worry, kid."

She punched me in the arm. "Don't do that."

"Don't do what?"

Nicole had come back home. Neither of us had heard her. Dolores said, "Mark was just annoying me."

"Was he now? He annoys me all the time."

"Are you going out again?" I asked Nicole.

She looked at me before walking over to open the fridge, taking out a bottle of water. I glanced at Dolores, who shrugged her shoulders.

Nicole closed the fridge, opened the water, and took a long drink. She looked at Dolores and asked her, "What do you feel like for dinner tonight?"

She shrugged. "Don't know."

"I was thinking the three of us could go to the pub and get something."

"What about Mum?" Dolores asked.

"I was including your mum."

"What about Mark?"

"What about him?"

Dolores glanced at me with pleading eyes. I said, "Don't worry about it, kid. I have something I have to do tonight anyway."

"Like punch someone's lights out?" Nicole asked coldly.

I turned to Dolores. "Give us a minute, kiddo."

"Okay, but no fighting. Shit, I didn't mean that."

"Go on."

When she was gone, I said, "Okay, let me have it. No sense in keeping it bottled up. No good for the baby."

"Don't you even bring the baby into this conversation," Nicole snarled.

It was like taking a cork out of a bottle. Nicole gave me all of her bottled-up anger and then some. I stood there and took it because most of what she said was true, and for the other part, I wasn't game enough to speak. Must have been the color of her face. Besides, if I got caught later that night, I figured my life was forfeit.

I led with, "You're right. It was stupid, and I shouldn't have done it."

"Then why did you, Mark?" she asked.

"I got angry when I saw what he did."

"Did it not occur to you to tell me?"

"Babe, she was beaten because they're afraid she said something."

She looked at me like I was crazy. "What?"

"They're all involved, Nicole. I'm not exactly sure how, but someone killed Les Jones for his land and the copper that was on it. Doc Rendado, Brian Warner, the old mayor, Bass Crown, Barry Kendrick, Geraldine Robinson's grandfather—they were all involved. I'm not sure how, but it has something to do with the mine and the town."

"They're all dead, Mark."

"That generation, Nicole. But not this one."

"What are you on about?"

I put my hand up to my face and pinched the bridge of my nose. "Doc Rendado's death was suspicious."

"How, Mark? How was it suspicious? He got bitten by a snake while he was milking it."

"He was milking it at the wrong time of the day, and his snake stick was leaning against the wall, not where it should have been, Nicole. It doesn't add up."

Nicole sighed. "The coroner will decide that."

I was getting angry with her, and I had to take in

some deep gulps of air to calm down. She had to do things the logical way. She didn't have the luxury I had.

"Fine."

"Mark."

"It's fine. We'll see what the coroner says." I paused. "I can tell you what he'll say, Nicole. Death by fucking snakebite."

I turned and stalked toward the door. "Where are you going, Mark?"

"I have some things to look into."

"What time will you be home?"

"Late."

CHAPTER FORTY-SEVEN

I went to see Tracey at her caravan. It was dark, and she was sitting with just a dull lamp lit, watching her television. I knocked, and when she opened the door, she asked, "What do you want? I'm not taking any dicks tonight. Especially the private kind."

"Just came to see if you are all right," I replied. "How is the eye?"

"I'm fine."

"Can I come in?"

She turned away but left the door open. "Whatever."

I climbed the steps, and the van rocked under my weight. I sat down and regretted it immediately. This time I'd sat on a tube of lube. There was a small pop, and I felt a wet patch on my ass. "Shit."

"What do you want, Mark?"

"Why did he beat you?"

"I told you already."

"No, why?"

"Because he thought I'd told you something I shouldn't have. Something about his father."

"What about his father?"

"That's just it. I don't know, Mark. All I knew was what I told you. How he said he saved the town."

"But how did he save the town?"

"I don't know?"

She was anxious, and her voice became elevated.

"Okay, it's all right. On the other hand, I don't think Hal will touch you again."

"Oh no. What did you do?"

"Something I shouldn't have." I stood up. "I have to go."

Tracey hesitated before saying, "Mark, thank you. No one ever stood up for me like that before."

"Can I make a suggestion, Tracey?"

"What?"

"Get out of this town. Find yourself another line of work."

"Maybe one day."

———

This was the part of the evening where things got a little hairy. You'll see why. I went to the Last Stop Motel—a.k.a. the funeral home—and waited in the Monaro for a few minutes. I grabbed my small penlight and my lock picks and put on a balaclava before climbing out into the night. I'm not sure if it was the weather or me, but the evening air seemed to be super-heated.

Heading around to the side, there was a door that said "Deliveries." I figured this was where they brought in the soon-to-be dusty companions.

Placing my hand on the handle, I was surprised when it turned. Looking around furtively, I went inside, finding myself in a long hallway with a hard tiled floor. Using my penlight, I flashed it around as I walked along the wide corridor, my footsteps sounding like a bloody draft horse tromping along it.

I slowed my pace, dropping the volume of my passage to an annoying soft squeak, similar to what you'd hear walking through a hospital. I located the section designated for long-term inmates. The sign on the door said "Embalming Area."

Pushing through the swinging doors, I was met with the strong smells of bleach, disinfectant, and formaldehyde. In front of me was a steel tray, like a bed where they did their thing. Along the far wall was a series of stainless-steel doors to each body.

Crossing to the doors with the closest proximity, I began opening them. The first two contained older women, so not the ones I needed. The third door, I hit pay dirt. Sliding the drawer out, I came face-to-face with Bert Styles.

"Hello, Bert," I said nervously. "Hanging out with all your friends, I see."

I started checking him over with my penlight. I found the total sum of zero. However, I wouldn't be outsmarted. I knew Bert had been murdered, just not how. Then I found it. A small puncture mark just inside the hairline at the base of his skull. "Son of a bitch."

I reached for my cell and took a quick picture. I also took one of Bert just to prove that it was him. Then, I slid him back into his refrigerated home and closed the door.

———

I couldn't take what I knew to Nicole, so I took it to Hopetown's next best investigator. "Damn it, Mark. Do you know what time it is?"

Larry stared at me through sleep-bleary eyes. I

glanced at my watch. It was close to midnight. "It's only early."

"Some of us go to bed at a reasonable hour."

"Me too."

"Shit, come in."

I walked through the door into his small unit. "Sorry, Larry."

"You want a coffee?"

"Sure, why not?"

Larry took the time to make both drinks while I sat at his kitchen table on a matching chair. Both, I was certain, had come off the set of some fifties movie. Larry placed the cup in front of me and asked, "What do you want, Mark?"

Bringing up the photo I had taken earlier, I slid my phone across the table so he could see it. "What am I looking at?" he asked with a frown.

"That is evidence of murder."

"Whose?"

"Bert Styles."

He glanced up at me and asked, "How did you get this?"

"Not the right question, Larry. The right question is why someone wanted to kill him."

"Okay, why?"

"Because, my dear Watson, they were afraid someone would take his ramblings seriously," I explained. "Trouble is, someone listened to him."

"You?" Larry asked.

I nodded. "Me. Both he and Rendado were murdered."

"But who killed him?"

"Rendado. He was the only one who visited him right before he died. I'll bet my balls that he injected him with something. Then they killed Rendado to shut him up."

"Who killed Rendado?" Larry asked.

"The guys in the BMW. They arrive, and things happen. They threatened me, and they beat Eddie Jones to a bloody pulp."

"Eddie was beaten?"

"Yeah. He's in the hospital. You need to be careful, Larry. Did you find that link I was asking about?"

"I was waiting for the right time to tell you. I have nothing."

"That's okay. It's probably for the best." Then something else came to me. "What do you know about the motel owners?"

"Jarred and Alice?"

"Yes."

"Not much. Nice people, keep to themselves. Occasionally see them at the pub. Rarely together."

"Yeah, that's what I got."

"Why?"

"Just curious." I looked at the notepads on the table. "Bringing your work home?"

"I'm writing a piece on the Hopetown drug problem," he explained.

I vaguely remembered Nicole saying something about drugs. "*Is* there a problem?"

He made an indifferent movement with his head and pulled a face. "Maybe. But it's worth writing a short piece about it."

"What kind of drugs, Larry?"

He stared at me. "I'm really surprised that you don't know. You are living with a copper."

"One of those wasn't listening and nodding moments," I replied.

"Ice. A few of the young people have been caught with it. One overdosed."

"A few doesn't make an epidemic, Larry," I said.

He nodded. "Yes, but those are the ones we know about. For every one person that we know about, there are up to ten that we don't."

"Those are some pretty grim figures," I said.

"It's a sign of the times."

"Any idea on how the stuff gets into town?" I asked.

"No idea. Strangers. When you first mentioned the BMW, I thought that might be something, but obviously not."

"How long has it been coming in?" I asked after drinking the last of my coffee.

"A couple of months."

I frowned, deep in thought, then said, "I'd best be getting home. Big meeting tomorrow."

"Good luck with it."

"Yeah."

CHAPTER FORTY-EIGHT

Day 9, Wednesday

"What time did you get in last night?" Nicole asked.

"Late" was the one-word reply.

"What did you get up to?"

Oh, I broke into the funeral home and took pictures of a dead guy. "Not a lot."

Dolores said, "I think I might have to go get a coat. It's a little chilly in here this morning."

I turned and fixed my stare on her. "Dolores, go to school."

"Can't remember. I went Mike Tyson on that kid's ass."

"Good morning," Linda said as she walked in. "Beautiful day outside."

"If you say so," I grunted.

"Whoa, someone got off on the wrong side of the sofa."

"If you must know," I said. "I'm waiting for an apology from Beachball Barbie."

Nicole put her cup down. "Oh no, you did not just say that."

"You know Barbie is blonde, right?" Dolores said.

"*Go to school!*" Nicole and I both snapped in unison.

"But—"

Linda grabbed her daughter by the hand. "Come on. I'll buy you breakfast."

"From where?"

"The roadhouse."

The front door closed, and then we got down to business. "Okay, I'm sorry for calling you Beachball Barbie."

"So you bloody well should be," Nicole growled. "Just remember, you had a part in this too. A damn big part."

"I know, I know."

"So what is the problem?"

I shook my head. "Don't worry. It's fine."

"Fine, bullshit. Speak to me, Mark. I'm not going through the whole day wondering what I'm going to come home to later."

"I just feel like you don't listen to me at times."

"Are you talking about Doc Rendado's death?"

"Yes."

"I deal with evidence, Mark," Nicole said. "Facts and evidence. It's how we operate."

"I know, Nicole."

She sighed. It was one of those I'm going to regret this, ones. "Okay, tell me again."

"Someone is cleaning up loose ends," I said. "Doc Rendado was one of them."

"I'm listening, Mark."

"First, he always milked his snakes in the morning."

"He could have changed," Nicole said.

"Next, when you milked a snake, he never would have put the cage on the table where he worked. He would have left it on the floor or wherever it belonged. Add to that, his hook was leaning against the wall. There is no way he would wrangle that snake without it."

"Anything else?" Nicole asked.

"Yes. Catch."

While I'd been talking, I'd grabbed an apple out of the bowl on the table. It sailed through the air, and Nicole caught it in her right hand. "What was that, Mark?" She wasn't happy.

"You caught that apple with your right hand. Not your left. If I repeated that another ten times, you would do the same thing. Because you are right-handed."

"Yes, so?"

"Doc Rendado was bitten on the right hand."

Nicole nodded. "He was right-handed."

"No, he was left-handed. Why would he try to get the snake with his right?"

"I don't know."

"He wouldn't because he's left-handed. Something or someone caused him to get bitten. Now I'll add something else. As a snake handler, he would have anti-venene on hand. If he got bitten, why didn't he administer that and then call for an ambulance?"

"Because he couldn't," Nicole replied.

"And why couldn't he?"

"Because someone was stopping him."

"Exactly."

"Shit. We need his body gone over with everything," she said. "I'll reach out to the coroner."

"That's not all, Nicole. You need to have the coroner check Bert Styles's body as well."

"Why?"

"Because I believe Doc Rendado killed him."

———

When Geraldine Robinson arrived for our lunch date, she came with an escort. Two big men dressed in black suits, and even though I didn't see one, my guess was that they carried guns. At least I now knew where Tweedle Dum and Tweedle Dee in the BMW came from.

I was seated at the table, sipping a Coke while waiting for her to arrive. She was ten minutes late. Mr. Hayes?"

"Call me Mark," I replied.

"I'm Geraldine Robinson. Gerry for short."

She had long dark hair and wore tailored white slacks and a white blouse so sheer I could see her bra through it. She stared at me with brown eyes as though trying to read me. Or maybe it was a standover tactic to make me aware of the power she wielded.

Eventually, she sat down, and her friends moved to a table beside the window. Franky came out, and I said, "Shall we order, Gerry?"

The smile she gave didn't fool me. It was cold and calculating. She was quite attractive, actually. "Let's."

Gerry ordered salad and some other stuff that I can't pronounce. I was actually surprised that it was on the menu. Me, I just ordered my usual fare. Steak and chips. When Franky went to get the order of Gerry's two goons, they just shook their heads. I guess they'd filled up on steroids before arriving.

"Have you and your family been in Hopetown long?" Gerry asked me.

I grinned and shook my head. "You already know the answer to that question."

She gave me one of her smiles. "Yes, I do."

"Would you care for a drink?"

"Sure. White wine."

Taking my empty Coke glass, I went over to the bistro bar and ordered white wine for her and a beer for me.

Paying for it myself, I picked up the drinks and returned to the table. "Did your hired help want anything?"

Gerry shook her head. "No, they're fine."

"Fair enough."

"Shall we discuss what we're here for?" she asked.

"Not yet. Why ruin a good meal by talking business?"

"What should we talk about then?"

"You," I replied. "You seem to know all about me, but I know nothing about you?"

"Fine. Shoot."

"You married? Single? Children?" I started with the basics.

"Single, no children."

"Working girl," I surmised.

"If you mean married to the job, then the answer is yes."

"The mine is a family business, huh?"

"Yes."

"You live out this way or elsewhere?"

She gave me her *Are you crazy* look. "God, no. I live in Sydney. I only come out here when I need to check on something or there is a problem."

"Helicopter? Plane?"

"Plane. There is a strip at the mine."

I nodded. "Mine is worth a bit then?"

"About three billion."

"I'm impressed."

Our lunch arrived, and we started to eat. Gerry, like a mouse, picking at her food. Me, like the ravenous wolf that I am, tearing into the meat as though it were my last meal. I looked up to find that she was watching me. "Sorry. I'm hungry."

"I would never have guessed."

"Can I ask you a question?"

"Depends. I thought we weren't discussing business until after we ate."

With a shake of my head, I said, "No, nothing like that. Do you drug test your workers?"

Gerry nodded. "At least once a week."

"And they come into Hopetown on their days off?"

"The ones who don't fly home," she replied.

"Do you have any positive tests for ice?"

She frowned at me. "Why?"

"Call me curious," I replied.

"There has been an uptick over the past couple of months."

"Do you know where they're getting it?"

She shook her head. "Just bringing it in with them, I guess."

I stored the information away for later use. I finished my lunch not long after Gerry finished hers. I pushed the plate away and said, "All right, let's talk turkey."

"Leave this investigation alone." Her words were soft but firm.

"I was going to," I told her truthfully. "But then a few things happened, and I changed my mind. Like the deaths of two locals."

"A heart attack and a snakebite victim," Gerry said.

"Both were staged murders, Gerry. Someone is taking care of loose ends."

"Why would you say that?"

My guess is she was looking to see what I knew. "Rendado killed Bert Styles, and someone staged the snakebite scene to make it look like an accident. But they screwed up. My guess is it is two of your men in a BMW."

"And why would someone do that?"

"Bert Styles saw another rider out there the night Les Jones was killed—sorry, murdered. He was killed just in case he remembered something else. Rendado was killed because he was the one who falsified the death report. And he killed Styles to keep him quiet. Couldn't have that getting out. Now, I'm guessing all roads lead back to you and your billion-dollar operation."

"I'll give you a million dollars."

Bingo.

Gerry continued. "All you have to do is walk away and forget everything you think you know. The money will be a great help to you and your family."

"And if I don't?" I asked.

"I run a billion-dollar operation, Mark. If anything endangers that, I'm going to do whatever it takes to ensure that doesn't happen. On top of that, think of your family."

My face hardened.

"You're beginning to throw that family word around a bit carelessly, Geraldine," I said in a low voice. "Don't push me. You may not like what I'm capable of."

"I know all about you, Mark," she said confidently. "We aren't some bikers or a low-level criminal organization you can push around."

"Great, you can use a computer," I replied with an overt level of sarcasm.

Gerry rose to her feet. "Take the offer, Mark. I'll be waiting to hear from you. You will be a gentleman and get the tab, won't you?"

And then she was gone, along with her entourage. "Sure, not like I'm short of a dollar," I muttered to myself.

CHAPTER FORTY-NINE

The first thing I did after lunch was head home and call everyone together. Dolores was already there, and so was Linda. Nicole arrived home at a hundred miles per minute. I was surprised she didn't have her lights and siren going. "What is the big emergency?"

"I just had lunch with Geraldine Robinson," I informed them.

"Who?" Linda asked.

"Geraldine Robinson. She owns the Peak Vale Copper Mine."

"How did it go?" asked Nicole.

"She offered me a million dollars to drop the case."

"Did you take it?" Dolores blurted out.

I just stared at her.

She dropped her head. "No, of course not."

"The money isn't the issue," I said. "It's what came after."

"She threatened us, didn't she?" Linda said.

I nodded. "Yes, she did. It was veiled, but it was there."

"I'd best have a word with her," Nicole said.

"No," I replied firmly. "Just keep an eye out. I've decided to see this thing through to the end. Everyone is involved somehow, and I need to get to the bottom of it."

"Maybe I should take Dolores back to Sydney," Linda said.

"No," said Dolores. "I want to stay."

"She might be right, kid," I said.

"I won't go."

"You can come back once this is all over," Nicole said.

Dolores pouted. "You promise?"

"Sure."

"Mum?"

Linda nodded. "Yes, that's fine."

"You'll need a flight from Dubbo," I said.

"I'll organize it now," Linda replied as she grabbed her cell.

I turned to Nicole. "You two need to be careful as well."

"Are you sure there is a real danger, Mark?" Nicole asked.

"She more or less admitted to having Bert Styles and Rendado killed."

"Really?"

"Well, she didn't deny it."

A few minutes later, Linda finished and said, "We leave tomorrow."

"Okay. I will take you," I said.

"Are you sure?" Linda asked.

I nodded. "It's only a few hours there and back. What time do you need to be there?"

"One p.m."

"Okay, we'll leave here about eight."

"Thank you, Mark."

———

I grabbed the rifle and put it in the rear of the Monaro and then went to see Larry. He was beginning to get things ready for tomorrow's paper. He looked up and grinned when he saw me standing there. "How was lunch?"

"Oh, great. She offered me a million to drop the case and then threatened me."

"She sounds lovely."

"Yes."

"What are you going to do now?" Larry asked.

"I—"

The sound of a siren outside drew our attention. Larry looked at me and said, "Fire truck."

The newspaperman grabbed his camera and notepad and said, "Come on."

I don't know why, but I went. Maybe because I had no current plans, or maybe the fact that I was suspicious that the fire was connected to what I was looking into.

I was right. We followed the smoke, which wasn't hard to see, and found the Crown Real Estate building fully engulfed in flames.

I climbed out of the Monaro, and Larry got out on the other side. The fire boys were running around getting set. Suzie and Byron were already there, talking to Holly Crown. I moved closer so I could overhear what she was saying. "Called away to meet someone, but when I arrived at the address, there was no one there."

"Are you saying someone deliberately called you away and then lit the fire?"

"Would you say it's a coincidence?" Holly asked.

"Could be," Byron replied. "Wouldn't be the first time someone left an office and left something on. Were you cooking anything? Left the kettle on?"

"The kettle has an automatic shut-off, and why would

I have cooking facilities in my damn office?" Holly was becoming irritated.

"Have you had anyone come and see you in the past couple of days?" I asked.

"Yes, you."

"Mark, go away," Suzie said.

I ignored her. "Besides me. Anyone from out of town?"

She looked torn. "I—"

Holly stopped, gathered herself, then said, "Yes, two men came and asked about records pertaining to the sale of the Jones property years ago. Just like you."

"Can you describe them?"

She did. My friends from the BMW. Gerry had left a parting gift. "Thank you."

I glanced at Suzie, who just glared at me. I heard the crunch of tires on grit and turned to see Nicole pull up. She rolled out of the vehicle and looked around the scene. Then she saw me and came over. "Why are you here?"

"I came with Larry. Actually, not quite true. He came with me."

"Fine. You can leave now."

I thought about arguing the point, but decided against it. Instead, I said, "I'll see you tonight."

Approaching Larry, I asked him, "You right to get back to the office?"

"Are you going to tell me what's going on?"

"What do you mean?"

He nodded toward where Holly was talking to Suzie and Byron. "You were talking to them."

"Well, Larry, if I were a betting man, which I'm not, I'd say that Geraldine Robinson's thugs just burned the real estate office down to get rid of some evidence."

"The evidence on your phone?"

"That would be my guess," I replied.

"So," Larry said. "Bert Styles, Doc Rendado, and the real estate office. I wonder what's next?"

I stopped suddenly. "Shit, you're right."

"What is the one way to stop it all getting out?"

"Get rid of everyone and everything involved," Larry said.

With a nod of agreement, I said, "And who knows the most?"

"The Kendricks," Larry replied.

All I could think of was the little girl. "Come on, Larry."

"What?" he was surprised I was trying to drag him away. "I'm working here."

"If I'm right, and I pray that I'm not, there is a bigger story not far from here."

He thought for a moment and said, "All right. But if you're wrong, you buy every paper I print for the next year."

"If I'm wrong, Larry, I'll gladly do it."

CHAPTER FIFTY

But I wasn't wrong.

Tyrone Kendrick was lying in the yard near the machinery shed. He'd been shot in the chest and in the head. From what I could tell, he'd been working on something and come out to see who was there. Most likely, he'd heard a vehicle. There was a wrench beside him. After he'd been shot, someone had stood over him for the coup de grâce. It had happened earlier that day.

I grabbed the Winchester rifle from the back of the Monaro, jacked in a round, and looked at Larry. "Wait here. There is a SAT phone under the passenger seat. Call it in."

"What if they're still here?" he asked nervously.

"If they were still here, they'd be shooting at us."

"Have you been shot at before?"

I remembered Friar's Lake. "Yeah."

Starting toward the homestead, my nerves began to jangle. I had an idea of what I'd find, but I hoped it wouldn't be the little girl. Maybe she'd be in school, like her uncle.

Hesitating for several moments outside the door, I

pulled the screen, which screeched as though warning me not to enter. Placing my foot just over the threshold, I stopped. Mabel Hendrick lay a few feet in front of me. She'd been shot in the back while running away.

Beyond her was Henry, her husband. By the looks of it, he'd poked his head out of the kitchen and been killed right there. The door jamb behind his slumped body was painted red with blood.

Before I stepped over the woman, I checked her, and once I was certain she was dead, I moved on to Henry. When I reached him, I found him to be the same as the others.

The kitchen was empty, but the back door was ajar. Making my way through the rest of the homestead, I went in search of Emily. Thankfully, I couldn't find her.

Larry opened the front screen door, and I heard him gasp. I called out, "Stay there, Larry. I'll be with you in a moment."

I made my way back outside, finding Larry in the yard, his face pale. He saw me and shook his head. "Nicole and her people are on their way. The Kendricks. Are they all…"

"The adults. I can't see the little girl, and I assume she and the other son are in school."

"Ah, shit."

"We'll keep looking for the girl just in case. Her name is Emily."

Doing a thorough search around the homestead and sheds, we called out Emily's name. After twenty minutes, we still had nothing. I looked out across the flat, desolate plains around the house and saw emptiness.

Larry came back to me. "Do you think they took her?"

I shrugged. "I have no idea. Like I said, maybe she's in school."

"Why, Mark? Why would they do this?"

"Like I said. They needed to shut them up. They knew too much. The kicker here is, two kids have lost both parents."

"Both?"

"Yes. I'm reasonably sure that Grace Holland is dead too."

"What makes you think that?" Larry asked.

"Because if she were still alive, she would be in town. She wouldn't go anywhere her daughter wasn't. Which means she's either incapable, or she's dead."

Larry was about to say something when a chicken started squawking and raced out of the henhouse. I frowned and started toward it. "Come with me, Larry. I think I just found our missing child."

When we reached the henhouse, I passed him the rifle. "Don't shoot yourself."

I ducked low as I went through the opening in the pen's exterior. The smell of wet ground and chook shit was strong at the back of the pen where the henhouse was. It was made out of corrugated iron and wood.

As I got closer, I thought I heard something. I stopped and held my breath. There it was again. Singing. A little girl's voice.

My shadow filled the doorway of the henhouse. It must have scared her because there was a small yelp. I squatted down to make myself smaller. "Emily?"

I could see her backed into a dark corner. "Hey, Emily. Remember me? I was at the pub when you came for lunch."

She never spoke.

"Remember? You wanted raspberry."

"I remember."

"That's right. I'm going to help you," I said softly. "How about you come over here?"

She shrank back even further.

"Okay, I won't come any closer. The police are coming. They will be here soon. Okay?"

"Okay."

I didn't bother with asking her what happened. The poor child was traumatized enough. I had an idea. "Would you like something to eat?"

No response.

"I think I have chocolate in my car."

"Caramello Koalas?"

"How about Freddo Frogs?"

"Uh-huh."

I held out my hand. "Come on, I'll take you to it."

She shrank back even further.

"How about I bring it to you?"

"Yes, please."

"I'll be right back."

I retraced my steps back out into the yard. I'd lied about the frogs. Now I needed to improvise. Larry was waiting. "Is she okay?"

"Looks to be," I replied, starting for the house.

"What are you doing?"

"Working a hunch."

Back in the house, I traipsed over the crime scene once more. I'd deal with the fallout later. Some things are more important. In the kitchen, I opened the refrigerator. I don't know what I expected to find, but there they were, sitting on the second shelf.

I grabbed the packet of chocolate koalas and went back outside. I removed one and handed the bag to Larry. "Hold these."

Returning to the henhouse, I called out, "Hey, Em, I'm back."

"Did you get a frog?"

I held it out. "No, I did one better and got your koala."

Emily came forward and took it from my grasp. She tore it open and put the lot inside her mouth.

"Good?"

"Yes."

"Would you like more?"

"Uh-huh."

This was the test. "Come with me, and I'll get them for you."

"Is he gone?"

"Who, sweetie?"

"The man," Emily replied. "Is he gone?"

"Yes." I assumed she meant the men in black. Maybe she saw only one of them.

"I saw him hurt Grandma. And I ran out through the kitchen."

"It's okay. You don't have to talk about it," I told her, holding out my hand.

Surprisingly, this time, she took it. I led her outside, but before we left the chicken pen, I said, "I'm going to pick you up, Emily. Just close your eyes, and I'll take you to my car. I'll give you some more chocolate there."

"Okay."

She was tentative, but let me do it. I carried her to the Monaro, talking quietly as we went. Larry followed us over. I put her inside and said, "Just stay here, okay?"

"Yes."

Larry passed me the packet, and I handed it to Emily. As she began tearing wrappers, Larry and I moved away. "Is she okay?" he asked again.

"Traumatized," I replied. "She saw Mabel killed."

"Where's my dad?" Emily called out.

"He'll be here soon," I lied. I glanced helplessly at Larry. "How the hell do you tell her?"

"Leave it to the professionals."

———

The police cars appeared first, followed by the ambulance. Nicole climbed out of her vehicle and came over to me. "Shit, Mark, what happened here?"

I pointed to Tyrone Kendrick. "From what I can gather, Tyrone was killed first. Then Mabel. She's in the hallway. Emily saw her die, poor kid. She ran out through the kitchen and hid in the chook house. Henry Kendrick is in the house too."

"Where is Emily?"

"In the Monaro, eating chocolate koalas."

Nicole turned. "Suzie?"

Suzie looked at her boss.

Nicole pointed toward my ride. Suzie nodded and went over to it. She squatted beside the door and started talking to Emily. Nicole turned her attention back to me. "Why the hell are you here, Mark?"

"We figured that they would try to tie up loose ends."

"We?"

I pointed to Larry. "Poor guy has never seen anything like this before."

Nicole shook her head. "Okay, now tell me who they are."

In the background, Byron and Paul were doing their best to secure the crime scene. I said, "Men in black. That's what Emily said. But she says she only saw one."

"Men in black? This is not some kind of fucking movie, Mark." There was a hint of anger in her voice.

"The guys in the BMW," I told her. "It has to be them. While I dined with Geraldine Robinson, she had her people out here taking care of business."

"Why?"

"I'm going to find out," I replied.

"No. You stay away from this. I'll have Suzie take

statements from you both, and then you go home." She sighed and looked at her watch. "I'm going to be out here forever. The detectives will be arriving in a couple of hours. I need to set up some lights before they do. Fuck."

"Has someone let young Jake know?"

"He's being kept at the school. I've called for homicide detectives and for a psych. God knows they're going to need them." Her eyes bored into my soul. "How are you?"

"You know. Nothing I haven't seen before."

"Just talk if you need to."

"Yes, Mum."

"I'm serious, Mark."

"Yeah."

For the next hour, Larry and I were stuck at the crime scene waiting to have statements taken. In that time, a welfare officer arrived and took Emily into town. Once we were done, I said to Larry, "You coming?"

"Where?"

"To get something to eat."

"Yes."

CHAPTER FIFTY-ONE

I arrived home late to find Dolores and Linda packing. Larry and I had gone to the pub and wasted money on meals. By the time we left, they were both untouched. Word had spread like wildfire about the murders at the Kendricks' property.

At one point, I'd received a text from Nicole telling me that one of the detectives was coming into town and wanted to talk to Larry and me. We were to meet at the station. Paul was bringing him in. The detective was one of three who had been flown in.

Arriving early at the station, we had to wait five minutes until Paul arrived with the detective. As they alighted from the police Land Cruiser and escorted us both inside, Paul said, "You'll go first, Mark."

Ushered into the interview room, where everything was recorded verbally and visually, I sat down opposite the detective. It was a woman. My guess was that she was given the shit job. But what did I know? Dressed in a tan pantsuit, she had her blonde hair tied back in a severe bun.

"My name is Detective Constable Heather Stroud. You are..."

"Mark Hayes. Private investigator."

"Wouldn't have thought there would be much call for a PI out here." Her tone was condescending. She'd already put me into the wannabe cop basket.

"You'd be surprised." I was in no mood for being a smartass.

"Okay. Let's start with why you went out to the Kendricks' property?" Stroud said.

"I had a hunch something bad was going to happen after the others."

"What others?" Stroud's brow furrowed.

"Bert Styles and Doc Elias Rendado."

"What happened to them?"

"They were murdered."

"Why do you say that?"

"Doc Rendado gave Bert Styles a hotshot to make it look like a heart attack. Rendado was killed by a snake."

"That can hardly be murder."

"It is if it was deliberate."

"Do you have any evidence?" Stroud asked.

"It's there if you look."

"I'm sure." She sounded doubtful but continued. "Who would want to murder them?"

"The same person responsible for the deaths of the Kendricks."

"Who might that be?"

"Geraldine Robinson," I replied.

"Do you have any evidence?"

"She has men in town. They drive a BMW. They wear black."

"Do you have any proof, Mr. Hayes?"

"No, but it has to be them. The little girl saw them."

"No, the little girl saw a man."

"I'm telling you, it has to be her. She already warned me off the case I'm working on."

"What case might that be, Mr. Hayes? A lost calf?"

Okay, now I was getting angry with the snide comments. "No, it was a bloody thirty-year-old murder."

"Calm down, Mr. Hayes."

I stared at her.

"What murder are you talking about?"

"It doesn't matter," I replied.

Stroud sighed. "If you say so. Tell me what happened when you arrived at the Kendricks' property."

"We found Tyrone face down in the yard."

"Who is we?"

"Me and Larry," I replied.

"And that would be Tyrone Kendrick?"

"Yes."

"Before I go on, I was made aware that you were acquainted with Tyrone Kendrick. Is that right?"

I glanced at Paul. He looked guilty. "Yes, that's right."

"Was it a civil relationship?"

"If you mean by civil, were we friends? The answer is no. He was a wife-beating asshole. He was also violent toward other people."

"Yes or no would suffice."

"No."

"Why was that?"

"Because he—what has this got to do with what happened?"

"Just getting some background, Mr. Hayes."

"Uh-huh."

"Tell me what happened next."

I said, "I got concerned about the little girl."

"Emily Kendrick?"

I nodded.

"Say it aloud for the recording, Mr. Hayes."

"Yes."

"You weren't concerned about the others?" Stroud asked.

"No."

"Why not?"

"Because I knew they were already dead," I replied. "I just hoped the little girl was at school, like her uncle."

"But she wasn't."

"No."

"Tell me what you found."

"I found Mabel dead in the hallway."

"That would be Mabel Kendrick? Correct?"

"Yes."

"Go on."

I continued. "She had been shot. Emily saw it happen."

"Did she tell you that?"

"Yes."

"Thank you. Please continue."

"I checked Mabel to make sure she was deceased. Once I'd established that, I saw Henry Kendrick lying half out of the kitchen."

"And he was dead too."

"He'd been shot in the head. His bloody brains were on the doorjamb."

Stroud nodded. "What happened next?"

"I went back outside. I assumed the little girl—"

"Emily," Stroud interrupted.

"I assumed Emily wasn't there. But something scared one of the chickens, and I went to check it out."

"Why?"

"Why, what?"

"Why did you go to check it out?"

"Because something startled one of the hens."

"So you checked it out."

"Yes."

"What did you find?" Stroud asked.

"The little girl—"

"Emily."

Damn, she was getting annoying. "Emily was hiding inside. Backed into a dark corner."

"What happened when she saw you?"

"She was tentative. I tried to coax her out, but she wouldn't come."

"How did you get her to come out?" Stroud asked.

"Chocolate koalas."

"I can see how that would work."

"She eventually came out, and I put her in the car. By that time, Nicole and—"

"Sergeant Berger."

"Was already on the way."

"There was no sign of anyone else there at all?" Stroud asked.

"No."

"Nothing that stood out?"

"Apart from the bodies?"

There was sarcasm there, which she chose to ignore. "Yes."

"I think I saw Elvis."

She ignored that too. "I think that will do for the moment. Don't leave town."

Standard fare. "And go where? Mind you, I do have to go to Dubbo tomorrow."

"What for?"

I told her.

Stroud shook her head. "Make other arrangements."

"Really?"

"Really."

And we were done.

Which brings me back to arriving home and finding Linda and Dolores packing.

"Sorry, I'm restricted to town for the time being," I told them. "I'll find someone to take you."

Linda shook her head. "We'll stay."

"Yesss!" Dolores exclaimed.

"You do know there was a mass murder in town today?"

"We heard, but it's been decided. We're staying."

"Fine, explain that to Nicole."

Dolores stared at me. "Are you okay, Mark?"

I sighed. "Been a rough day."

She came over and wrapped her arms around me. "This'll help."

It didn't, but it was a wonderful gesture.

CHAPTER FIFTY-TWO

Day 10, Thursday

Nicole came in at some ungodly hour, kissed me on the forehead, and went to bed. I was gone by the time she was up and off to see Larry. When I arrived, he was putting the finishing touches on a follow-up story from the previous day's murders. I took one look at him and said, "You look like shit."

"I was up all night working on the story about the murders. It had to be done, ready to go out at four."

"How would you like to add to it today?" I asked him.

"What do you have in mind?" Larry asked.

"I need answers," I told him. "The only way to get them is to go to the one I figure is the weakest link."

"Who is that?"

"Mayor Hal Warner. Are you in?"

"Hell, yes."

———

The Monaro roared as it pulled up outside the mayor's office. Before I got out, my phone buzzed. It was a message from Nicole.

Where are you? Matt Stone never arrived in Dubbo. I'm going to work.

I ignored it. Yes, I know, my bad. But Stone was the least of my problems, probably off humping some backpacker he picked up on the way home.

I slammed my door and walked briskly toward the front door. Larry, surprisingly, followed close behind. He was as keen as I was for answers.

When I hit the swinging door, it crashed back. The receptionist was behind the counter, a startled expression on her face. "Is he in?"

"Yes, but—"

That was all I needed to know. The door made the original hole bigger as it crashed back. I strode around the desk toward the suddenly frightened mayor. I dragged him from his chair and slammed him down onto his desk. "Right, you fucking asshole, time to answer some questions."

"What are you doing?" he blurted out.

I slapped his face. "I'm doing the asking."

Larry closed the door.

"Do you know where I was yesterday, Hal? Huh? No? I was at the Kendricks' property. They're dead. Tyrone, Henry, and Mabel. All dead. But I guess you already know that. The whole fucking town knows. I found the little girl hiding in the henhouse. Now, you are going to tell me what's going on, or I'm going to bash your brains in with that fucking stapler beside you."

"Take it easy, Mark," Warner stammered.

"Be fucked. Let's start at the beginning. What happened to Les Jones?"

"I-I can't. She'll kill me."

I picked up the stapler.

"Okay, okay. My father killed Les Jones."

"Was he the rider that Bert Styles saw?" I asked.

"Yes."

"Why was he killed?"

Warner swallowed. "The copper. The sale of Les's property would help save the town."

"How?"

"Shares. Of the shares in the mine we were given, we were to keep 10 percent of the profits, and the rest would go into the town. It was a verbal agreement with Gordon Robinson."

"So what happened?"

"Nothing, it's still in place. It is still used to keep the town running."

"What happened to Ike Smith? He didn't look like he was going too well."

"The value of copper started to tank. The buyers were sourcing it from other places. Over time, the money got less and less. So much so, he was getting less than it took to keep him afloat. It was all right for Kendrick, because he had a good income. Ike didn't. I still have a job, so that was fine. I still put my money into the town. It's not a lot, but it gets us by."

"So that's what brought Geraldine Robinson out here?" I asked. "The mine is in trouble, and a scandal will bury it."

Warner nodded. "She is looking to get a bigger deal in China. Any trouble and the deal falls through, and Peak Vale goes tits up. Billions lost."

"So now that I'm looking into it, Geraldine is tidying up her grandfather's mess. Afraid I might find something. Bit fucking late for that."

"Oh god," Warner whispered.

"Doc Rendado killed Bert Styles, correct?"

Warner nodded. "Geraldine ordered it because she was afraid he might remember something."

"Then she had him killed too."

"Yes, because he wrote the false report."

I shook my head. "Nothing like a heart attack and a workplace accident to cover something up. So Les Jones was murdered because he wouldn't sell?"

"Yes. You must understand the town was dying. If the mine hadn't come, it would have been a ghost town within two years."

"Ike Smith was approached by Kendrick to buy the land from Jones's wife, but using Kendrick's money," I said.

This time, there was a shake of the head. "No, it was mine money. At the time, Barry Kendrick was going down with the ship like the rest of us. One bad season and all that."

"So how did it all come about? Who decided that Les Jones had to go?"

"They all did. My father, Barry Kendrick, and Gordon Robinson. Robinson wanted it all back then. He couldn't see past the dollar signs."

"How did Ike Smith get roped in?"

"Kendrick went to him after the funeral and told him how it was. Not the murder part, just the town needed money, and how much he could make from it. He didn't want to, but knew that if he didn't, he would lose everything."

"How do you know all this?" Larry asked.

Warner stared at the newspaperman. "My father told me before he died."

"The men in black," I said. "Are they Geraldine's people?"

"Yes."

"Did they kill Rendado?"

"Yes."

"You know they'll come for you before they're done, right?" I pointed out. "Does she know that you know all of this?"

He nodded. "I'm just waiting for the sword to drop."

I stared at him. Something didn't gel. If Geraldine knew what was happening, why hadn't she ordered her people to terminate him? In the grand scheme of things, Warner was the only one left.

I shrugged it off. The man was a weasel. "Expect a call from the police eventually."

As I left his office, I walked through the foyer. On the wall was a photo I'd never noticed before. In it were Warner, Ike Smith, Henry Kendrick, and Doc Rendado. All four were holding handguns. I read the inscription beneath. It said, "Hopetown Pistol Team, District Finals."

I looked at the woman behind the desk. "Pretty good shooters, huh?"

She looked at me warily. "Ah, yes."

"Was Hal out at all yesterday?"

A frown. "No."

"Thanks." I walked toward the door, Larry in tow.

"But he was late into the office."

I hesitated. "Thank you."

Walking out into the bright sunshine, Larry and I climbed into the Monaro. I pulled out of the parking lot and parked across and down the street a little. Larry stared at me. "What are we doing?"

"Something isn't right," I replied, shaking my head.

"How do you mean?"

"Why haven't they come after Warner?" I asked. "He was holding something back. Nothing gels. You heard all the information he had. If they were tidying up loose ends, I would have expected him to be one of the first."

"I can think of a reason," Larry said. "Although I don't want to think about it."

"I'm listening."

"His father killed Les Jones to protect the town—get it back on its feet, if you like. What if he passed it on to his son?"

"You mean made him responsible for the town's survival?"

Larry nodded. "Yes. Emily said one man. We assumed that there were two, and she didn't see two. What if it was just one?"

"You mean he was the one who killed Kendrick and his family? He's too timid. Philanderer, yes. Murderer? I'm not so sure."

"He uses a handgun. It would explain why he is still alive."

I thought about what Larry was saying. Yes, Warner could have killed the Kendricks. But what about Rendado and Bert Styles? I said, "It's possible. But that leaves Rendado and Bert Styles."

"He could have been behind Rendado's death too."

"How does he get him to put his hand in the snake box?" I asked out loud.

"A gun to his head," Larry surmised.

I shook my head. "Getting shot or snake bit. I know which way I'd choose to go."

"Okay. Just a theory. He would have anti-venene on hand, being a snake handler, right?"

"I guess so."

"What if he thought after getting bitten, he could save himself?"

"Plausible. But what happened?"

"What if he couldn't get to it?"

"He wasn't tied in any way," I said.

"What if it wasn't there? It would have to be close by in his snake room."

I reached for my cell. I hit the speed dial and waited.

"This better be important," Nicole said. "I'm bloody busy."

"Was there any anti-venene in the doctor's home?"

"What?"

"anti-venene. Doc Rendado should have had it on hand. I don't know why I didn't think of it."

"Mark, we talked about this. We both agreed that someone was stopping him."

"Humor me, Nicole. Was there any or not?"

"I don't know. I don't have the report from the scene."

"Okay, thanks." I disconnected the call before she could ask me why.

"We're going to have to go to Rendado's," I told Larry.

"Why?"

"I need to see if the anti-venene is there."

"Okay."

I was about to start the Monaro when Warner appeared. He looked nervous. "What's he up to?"

Warner climbed into a dark blue 4x4 and reversed out of his parking space. Then he pulled onto the street and started out of town. "Are we going to follow him?" Larry asked.

"Yes, I do think we should."

The Monaro roared to life, and I did a U-turn. Now, I'm not some kind of specialist when it comes to following someone, but Warner wasn't too worried about being followed. Or he was, but couldn't see the leaves for the trees.

He drove out of town and down toward the river. When we were almost there, I pulled off into some scrub and killed the motor. Then I grabbed the rifle, and we started for the river through the bush.

Crouching in the bushes at the edge of the riverbank, we saw Warner down in the sandy bottom digging a hole with his hands. Moments later, he grabbed a plastic bag with something inside and added to its contents.

Larry and I watched in silence as the mayor filled the hole in, sealing whatever was in the bag inside. Warner came to his feet and looked around before coming up out of the river and disappearing. A few minutes later, we heard the 4x4 start and leave the river.

"What do you suppose was in that bag?" Larry asked me.

I got to my feet. "Let's go and find out."

We walked down the bank and out to where Warner had buried the item. I dropped to hands and knees and began to dig. The earth was soft where it had been disturbed, and it didn't take much effort to dig up the bag and what was inside it.

Once it was clear of the riverbed, I opened the bag. Inside was a handgun. That was what Warner had been burying. I wrapped it back up, being careful not to touch it. "What are you going to do with it?" Larry asked me.

"Take it. Give it to Nicole."

"Shouldn't we leave it?"

He was right. But I wasn't going to put it back. "Come on, let's go."

"Where are we going?" Larry asked.

"Going to see a man about a gun."

CHAPTER FIFTY-THREE

Returning to the council building once more, we entered the mayoral office without knocking. Warner was red in the face from his sojourn to ditch the weapon in the riverbed. He looked up suddenly. An exasperated expression crossed his face. Then he saw what I held in my hand, and he went pale.

"I guess you know what this is?" I asked.

He shook his head slowly. "I have no idea."

"I'm guessing," I said, "that hidden away in this plastic bag is the murder weapon used to kill the Kendricks family."

Warner shook his head again, more vehemently. "I still have no idea what you mean."

"You see, we followed you. Out to the river. Then, while we watched, you buried it in the riverbed."

I didn't know it at the time, but Larry had his phone out and was recording the conversation we were having. If a man could lose all color in an instant, going from pale to snow white, it was Warner. "I—"

"It was you who killed the Kendricks, wasn't it? I

mean, I already know the answer, and ballistics on this weapon will prove it, but I want to hear it from you."

Surprisingly, he nodded. "I couldn't let him do it."

"Do what?"

"He was getting nervous about all the questions. He was going to withdraw all his money from the town, hoping that everything would just go away. But if he did that, the town would die. There would be nothing left."

"So you killed him just for that?"

"It was all right for him. He still had his property. Once the town was gone, I would have nothing. My father entrusted the town to me. It was my responsibility to fix everything."

"But you killed Rendado and had him kill Styles."

"Geraldine Robinson ordered Styles to be killed," he replied. "And she also wanted Doc Rendado gone as well. He was starting to get nervous while you were asking all the questions. He didn't think that you'd put it all together, but as soon as you came to him about the head wound, he knew it was only a matter of time. The silly old fool. He wanted to come clean."

"So you got rid of Rendado as well?" I asked.

"Yes."

"How did you do that?" asked Larry.

Warner looked at the newspaperman. "You know, I thought that was the easiest one of the lot. I figured that his getting bitten by a snake would have solved everything."

"Well, you fucked that up," I said. "For starters, he was bitten on the wrong hand. He never milked in the evening. And the wrangling stick, or whatever you call it, was against the wall. What I want to know is how he allowed himself to be bitten?"

"I held a gun to his head. He had a choice: bullet in the brain or get bitten by the snake. He chose the snake."

"Because he had anti-venene on hand?" I asked.

Warner half smiled. "But he didn't. Just before he got home, I had already broken in and removed it. He tried to find it, but it was long gone. I was still there waiting for him when he arrived from the care home."

"So that is why Geraldine Robinson hasn't killed you yet. You're tidying up the mess for her."

"Something like that."

"You do know that you know too much to keep on living, right?" I said.

"She assured me nothing would happen."

"Yeah, and pigs fly too."

Warner remained silent.

"It's over," I said.

It seemed to take a while for my words to register. Then something strange happened. He smiled. "You don't understand, do you?"

"What do you mean?"

"While you have been doing all your running around this morning, Geraldine Robinson had her men pick up the woman and the girl they've been watching." He held out his hand. "I'll have the gun. It's over for you."

"You're lying, Warner," I said. Yet I had a strange feeling that he was telling the truth.

He reached into his pocket and took out his phone. He flicked through with several swipes, then opened what he was looking for. He turned the phone around. I could see that it was a message. The name on it was Gerry.

It said: **We have the woman and the girl. Get rid of the gun, and we'll take care of the rest.**

As though on cue, my phone buzzed. Sick of hearing the witch's laugh, I'd had it on silent since then. I took it out and stared at the screen. There was a message. I opened it. The number had been blocked, but I already knew who it was from. There was a picture of Linda and

Dolores. They had gags over their mouths, and they both looked scared. Underneath the photo was a message.

Meet me at Granite Rock. Two hours. Come alone, no police. Or they die.

I showed Larry the message. "Oh shit."

"My thoughts exactly."

"They'll kill you."

"That would be my guess."

I sent a message back.

I have Warner. We trade.

It was a useless gesture because I was sure that he would be killed anyway. The cell buzzed.

Sure, bring him along.

Warner smiled like he'd won the lottery. Nope, wasn't having that. I walked around the desk and hit him. He staggered back and hit the wall. I grabbed him before he could slide to the floor. "Stop grinning, asshole. Guess what, you're coming with me. And before they kill me, I'm going to kill you."

"You won't get the chance, Hayes. I'm going to ask Gerry if I can do it. Up close, grinning my fucking ass off."

I hit him again. This time he slid down the wall and stopped at the floor. Dragging Warner to his feet, I rammed him back against the wall for good measure. When I spoke next, my face was only centimeters from his. "We're going to walk out of here like there's nothing wrong. If you try anything, you won't make it to the meet. Do you understand?"

"I won't say anything, Hayes. I wouldn't miss this for the world."

CHAPTER FIFTY-FOUR

We drove straight out to Granite Rock and prepared. I took the rifle and the box of bullets I had and looked over the terrain. The landscape was red with boulders to the west, the largest of which was called Granite Rock. The brush was sparse and stunted, and to the east, a dry creek with steep sides cut through the flat.

"What do you think?" Larry asked.

I had tried to get him to stay in town, but he wouldn't hear of it. He was obviously having more fun than he'd had in a while. Had to admire him for that. I said, "I have a plan, but you're not going to like it."

"How about you tell me, and I'll judge for myself?"

I told him. Larry shook his head and said, "Yep, that's totally shit."

"You in?"

"Hell, yes."

"Good. In the rear seat of the Monaro is a cowboy hat. When they come, put it on and pull it down low so your face is in shadow. It should give me enough time to go to work."

"Just don't mess it up." He cocked his head to one

side. "What about Warner? He'll start howling as soon as they arrive."

"Hold that thought." I went to the trunk and found an oily rag. "This should do."

We dragged the mayor from the back of the Monaro. His hands were already bound. "What are you doing?"

I tied the rag around his head, using it as a gag. Then I said to Larry, "When they arrive, get him out of this side. That will put the Monaro between you and them. If you need to, grab the handgun."

"The murder weapon?"

"Any port in a storm, Larry. Just remember to keep your head down."

I heard a crow in the distance. Its caw sounded like someone laughing at us. Maybe it knew something we didn't. Shoving Warner back into the car and satisfied with our impromptu plan, I said to Larry, "Keep your head down."

"Don't miss," was all he could say.

———

Any normal person looking to hide would have chosen the rocks. Not me. The dry creek offered a better field of fire where they would be when they turned up. I know, some of you may think that my shooting from cover without warning might seem like murder, but remember who these people are. The woman had already ordered the murders of two people, and those were the ones we knew about. Her thugs had beaten the shit out of the guy who'd hired me, and this whole mess started with another murder thirty years earlier. Now, there was no way they were going to let me walk away. Their plan would be to kill me and leave me out here for the wild dogs and dingoes.

No, stuff that. They didn't deserve a chance. Out here, it was kill or be killed. And I sure as shit wasn't about to let that happen. Not when I had a baby on the way.

The sun was high in the sky, and it was bloody hot. The cicadas were picking up their tempo, and I could feel the sweat running down my back. I muttered, "Shit, Mark. Here we are again. Remember what happened last time?"

Oh yeah, Friar's Lake, when I was involved in a gunfight with people who were robbing an armored car. That was the time when someone had shot Nicole as well. It was a miracle I still had her, let alone her going back to work.

With fifteen minutes to go, I sent Nicole a text message. She responded to it almost immediately.

WTF!

I waited.

My phone buzzed. It was Nicole. "Hello, beautiful."

"Mark, what's happening?"

"We have a little situation. You might want to roll everything you have out to Granite Rock."

"Okay, Mark. Now you're scaring me. Talk to me."

I told her what had happened and what I was doing.

"You damned fool, Mark. You damn, damn fool."

I could hear her voice breaking. I said, "I'll be fine, Nic. I'll get Linda and Dolores back safe and sound."

"And what about you? We need you safe and sound too."

I could hear her voice wobbling with emotion, her breathing growing heavy. She was hurrying somewhere. I heard her call out, "Suzie, get in the Land Cruiser. We're headed to Granite Rock. Paul, get the detectives and follow us. Shit is about to hit the fan. Vests and shotguns."

That's my girl, always prepared.

"Mark, are you still there?"

"I'm here, babe."

"How the fuck do you get into these things?"

"I often ask myself these things, Nic. I guess I'm just lucky."

I heard an engine. I looked up and saw that it wasn't one, but two vehicles. Dust spewed up behind them on the dirt road. "Hey, babe, I have to go."

"Mark, no, you can't—" Nicole's voice finally broke.

"Love you and little Jess."

"Wait!"

"I have to go, Nic."

"How did you know?" she asked. "How did you know I was having a girl?"

"Private investigator," I replied and disconnected.

Pocketing my phone, I picked up the Browning and jacked a round into the breech. Using the scope, I tracked the progress of the vehicles coming in. The BMW was in the lead, and the second vehicle was a black Range Rover.

They slowed to a stop around thirty feet from the Monaro. I used my phone to call Larry. "Yeah?"

"Leave the line open so I can hear what they say," I said to him.

"I got it, Mark."

Five people climbed out of the vehicles. Larry got out of the Monaro but kept it between himself and Gerry's people like I'd told him. Gerry stepped forward. "Nice hat, Mr. Hayes."

Larry remained silent.

"Where is Warner?" Gerry called out.

I focused on Larry. He remained silent but got Warner out of the Monaro. He was still gagged, and Larry held him there.

I heard Geraldine call out, "Send him this way."

"Don't do it," I muttered to myself.

Larry held him back.

"Send him this way," Geraldine called again.

Instead of speaking, Larry stabbed a finger at their vehicles. Geraldine turned and spoke to one of her men. He went to the back of the Range Rover and opened the door.

I watched as Linda and Dolores were dragged out. They were fine. Not safe, but fine. Beside where I lay, my cell buzzed like an angry bee. It was Nicole. It had to be, but I wasn't going to let myself be distracted.

Geraldine called out, "Start Warner over. We'll start the other two."

It sounded like the script of an old western movie I'd once seen. I think it was called *Rio Bravo*. John Wayne was in it.

Linda and Dolores began walking. Larry sent Warner going the other way. Watching them start to converge, I intended to wait until they reached Larry, and then I would open fire.

I never got the chance. Geraldine had other ideas.

While I watched, she turned her head and spoke to a big guy with a beard standing beside her. Before I knew what was happening, he'd taken out a handgun and fired.

Hal Warner stumbled and fell to the ground like a marionette with the strings cut. I let out an audible "Shit!" and fired.

The Remington slammed back against my shoulder as the .270 Winchester round streaked across the open ground. I saw the impact of the bullet in the side of Bearded Man's face. Blood and shit splattered Geraldine Robinson, covering her face and pale clothes.

As I worked the lever on the rifle, I called out, "Larry, tell them to run!"

Through the phone as I lined up another of Geraldine's men who was reaching for a weapon, I heard Larry shout, "Run! Run!"

The rifle in my hands whiplashed again. The guy who'd been reaching for his weapon staggered but never fell. Hurriedly, I levered in another round and fired again. This time, he went down hard.

By now, the two remaining bodyguards had forgotten all about Linda and Dolores. They ran for shelter behind the Range Rover, taking a stunned Geraldine with them. I caught sight of Linda and Dolores taking cover with Larry. I said, "Are they all right, Larry?"

"They're fine."

"Keep them there."

Suddenly, the sound of automatic gunfire hammered out across the landscape. Bullets stitched a line in the red dirt in front of me. I ducked down and heard the first weapon joined by a second. However, this time the fire wasn't directed toward me.

Across the gap, I could hear the staccato sound of bullets peppering the Monaro. Over the cell, I could hear cries of alarm. I came back up and saw a shooter leaning across the hood of the Range Rover. I fired at him, and the bullet skidded off the hood near his position.

"Shit!"

I was empty. That was the trouble with the Remington only having a 4-round magazine. I slipped back down and started to reload. It seemed to take forever when, in fact, it took about a minute.

Meanwhile, the shooters were still firing. But when I came up, I saw something troubling. One of the shooters had broken cover and was advancing on the Monaro. Larry and the others were hunkered down and had no chance of seeing.

"Larry, you've got a guy coming up on you."

I brought the rifle up and tried to get a bead on the bodyguard. He was moving too much. I fired, but the bullet flew wide. Then he was upon them.

Instead of the staccato sound of the automatic weapon, I heard a steady CRACK-CRACK-CRACK-CRACK. The bodyguard lurched under each impact from the handgun. As he staggered back, his finger depressed the trigger of his weapon, and a burst of fire was let loose. Over the phone, I heard a cry of pain and a female scream.

"Who's hit?" I demanded over the open line. "Talk to me. Who's hit?"

"Larry, Larry is shot."

It was Dolores.

"Where?"

"In the chest."

"Put pressure on the wound," I told her. "Use whatever you can find. Your hands if you must."

"O-Okay."

"And keep your bloody heads down."

With three down, Geraldine and her remaining man had a change of heart. They clambered back into the Range Rover and slammed the doors.

I heard the V-8 motor roar to life. As I came to my feet, the wheels on the vehicle were spinning on the dirt as it turned. I still had three rounds left in the Remington. I levered and fired until I was empty.

The Range Rover lurched to a halt, and the driver emerged, staggering away from the vehicle with limping strides. I reloaded once more. By then, the wounded man was a decent distance away with the Range Rover between us.

I jogged forward toward the Monaro. When I reached it, I saw Larry lying flat on his back. Dolores was pressing down on his chest to stem the flow of blood while Linda was on Larry's phone. "How is he doing?"

Dolores looked up at me with tears rolling down her cheeks. "I...I don't know what to do."

"Just keep doing what you're doing, kid. Keep the pressure up." I heard part of the conversation Linda was having. She was talking to Nicole, telling her she needed an ambulance.

"No, it's not Mark," I heard her say.

I glanced at the retreating bodyguard, then at the stationary Range Rover. The motor was still running. The bodyguard, not so much. He was slowing visibly. Then he fell to the ground. God only knew why he had abandoned the vehicle.

I walked over to the Range Rover. Geraldine Robinson was in the front passenger seat. She had been hit by one of my rounds. In the chest. Her blouse was all bloody, the fabric unable to soak any more, the blood staining her pants. Her breathing was shallow, blood running from the corner of her mouth.

Geraldine never moved, but her eyes found me. There was a question in them that I knew the answer to. I nodded and watched as the light in her eyes faded. Now there was only one left.

I started walking across the rock-strewn flat toward where the bodyguard lay. Gravel crunched beneath my boots, and for the first time, I noticed a tremor in my hands. The adrenaline surge was wearing off, and I was starting to realize what I'd just been involved in. "Hang in there for a few minutes more," I told myself.

When I reached the final bodyguard, he was dead. Like Geraldine, he'd been hit in the chest as well. The only difference was that he'd been able to run until he could run no more, and he'd fallen and died where he now lay.

My legs turned to jelly, and I sank to my knees. The gravel bit through my jeans into my knees. It was finally over. I knew why Les Jones had been killed, and why, and who had done it. Now I would have to face the consequences of my part in it all.

The shaking grew worse, and I could feel tears in my eyes—not of sadness, but of relief that I would get to see my little girl grow up.

Gathering myself, I regained my feet and walked back to the Monaro. Dolores was still putting pressure on Larry's wound. Linda looked up at me. "Are you okay, Mark?"

I nodded. "Yeah."

"What about the others?"

"All dead."

She shook her head. "Trouble just follows you around, doesn't it?"

"Yeah, it does."

I leaned against the Monaro and slid down until I was sitting. "How's he doing?"

"I think the bleeding is slowing," Dolores said.

"Good."

My eyes closed, and I listened to the sounds of the outback. I was still that way when Nicole arrived with the cavalry.

CHAPTER FIFTY-FIVE

I was reasonably sure that I was going to jail for murder. The detectives questioned me relentlessly about what had gone down, and they kept me in a cell for a couple of days. But as luck would have it, an old friend appeared.

When he entered the interrogation room, I looked up. At first, I was kind of shocked to see him, then I smiled. "Hello, Higgins."

"You, Mark Hayes, are an A-grade shit magnet."

Stewart Higgins and I had crossed paths before on a couple of occasions. He'd hauled me out of the shit more than once. In his hand was a folder, and when he sat down, he said, "How have you been, Mark?"

"You tell me."

Higgins opened the folder. Looking it over, he frowned. Then said, "You've been busy. Seven people shot. All but one of them deceased."

"In my defense, I only shot five of them." Larry had been airlifted to Dubbo after being stabilized. He was now on the mend.

"You're looking at serious time, Mark. Serious time."

"There wasn't much time to think about it, considering they were going to kill us all."

Higgins kept reading. "It says here, one of those killed was a mass murderer."

"I guess."

"Tell me in your own words everything that happened, from the beginning."

"A guy came to me and asked me to solve a thirty-year-old murder. I thought about it and told the client that I couldn't do it. I was under the illusion that it was an accident. Then I went to a rodeo and changed my mind."

"A rodeo?"

"Yes. You see—"

Higgins held up his hand. "I don't want to know."

"Okay. Anyway, I started asking questions, and two people died. Then the mayor killed three people out at the station. I found the little girl. There was no going back from there. As you know, it all culminated with the shootout at Granite Rock."

"This has just been a shitshow, Mark. By rights, I should let them throw the book at you. However, I'm going to let you go."

Suddenly, I felt relieved. But Higgins wasn't done with me. He said, "I don't work for the New South Wales Police anymore, Mark. I work with the feds. I have a special little task force, which could use a person like you."

"I'd rather not, Higgins," I said. "I have a kid on the way, and I'm needed around here."

"I'm not asking you to move from here, Mark. Think of this as a permanent part-time job. When I call on you, you come running. Or I can have you locked up on five counts of murder."

Shit. "When do I start?"

"Right now."

"Now?"

"That's right. Matt Stone."

"Ah, fuck."

Higgins grinned. There was no humor in it. "I heard there was a grievance between you two."

"Grievance? I'd like to punch him in the mouth. He came here on a missing person hunt and pissed off back to Dubbo when it got too hard."

"He didn't arrive in Dubbo. He was last seen here. I want you to find out what happened to him."

"Fine. On my own?"

"That's right. I don't have anyone else to spare."

"Shit."

With that done, Higgins left, and once he was gone, Nicole came into the interview room. She sat down opposite and stared at me. "Are you okay?"

I shook my head. "Did he tell you what he wants?"

"He did."

"Beats going to prison, I suppose."

Nicole reached out and grabbed my hand. This was the first time we'd been alone since the whole thing had kicked off. "I thought I'd lost you, Mark."

"I'm still here," I replied.

"How did it get to this?"

"Someone wanted me to solve a thirty-year-old murder."

"You should have come to me, Mark," Nicole said.

"I know, but they said no police. Besides, Larry and I had it covered."

"You almost got Larry killed," she pointed out.

"Don't remind me."

"Let's go home," she said.

I nodded. "Okay. Then you can fill me in on what happened to Matt Stone."

CHAPTER FIFTY-SIX

"Hey, you're home," Dolores cried as I walked through the door. She and Linda hadn't seen me since I was locked away in the Police Regency.

Dolores came over to me and wrapped her arms around my waist. "Easy, you'll break me."

"Don't care," she replied.

"Mind if I get in on the act?" Linda asked. "If you need a lawyer, I'm available."

I hesitated. "You sure you want to hug it out?"

"Oh, shut up and come here," she said, wrapping me in her embrace. "Thank you."

"I'd do the same for someone I liked," I said to her.

Linda stepped back and grinned at me. "Do you need me or not, Mark?"

I shook my head. "Nope, I'm free to go, as they say on TV."

She looked astounded. "Why—how?"

"I'll let Nicole tell you. I'm going for a shower."

Turning the water on as hot as I could stand, it felt like small needles piercing my skin. I let the water cascade from my head down to my toes and just stood there enjoying it. I had no idea how long I'd been in there when a voice said, "Are you getting out any time soon?"

Nicole stood there watching me. I hadn't even heard her come in. "I'm enjoying it."

"Get out. We need to talk."

I sighed and turned the water off. Once dry, I climbed into a pair of shorts and a T-shirt. Then I grabbed a beer from the refrigerator. Linda and Dolores had gone to bed.

As we sat together on the sofa, I said, "Tell me about Matt Stone."

"Not much to tell really," Nicole said. "He didn't show up in Dubbo. I've had our people looking around town, but he could have disappeared anywhere between here and his destination. Dubbo has had people out along the route, but so far they've found nothing."

"Not even his vehicle?"

"Not a trace."

I thought about Grace Holland. "Anything new on Grace?"

"No."

"Why me?"

"Because you're good at what you do."

"I hate being good at what I do," I replied.

"When you're finished, I might have to get you to help me," Nicole said.

"With what?" I asked.

"Finding out where all this ice is coming from."

I nodded slowly. "Larry was working on a piece for his paper on that. The strange thing is, when I had lunch with Geraldine Robinson the other day, I asked her about the stuff. She said testing results at the mine had gone up. It started about two months ago."

"It's something to look at, I guess."

"What will happen to Emily?"

"She'll go into care if her mother doesn't turn up."

"Jake?"

"He'll go into care no matter what." Nicole yawned. She leaned over and kissed me. "I'm going to bed. Love you."

"Love you too." Suddenly, I thought of something. "Wait. You said we're having a girl."

Nicole smiled. "Yes. But you knew that."

"Only had a feeling. What are we going to call her?"

"How about Olivia?"

I nodded. "That's nice. I like it."

I helped Nicole to her feet and watched as she waddled off to bed. Feeling too wound up, I decided to go back to work. Grabbing some paper, I began jotting down some notes about Matt Stone, the drugs, and Grace Holland. I wasn't giving up on her just yet.

CHAPTER FIFTY-SEVEN

Day 13, Sunday

I was asleep at the table when Dolores found me the next morning. She was the first one up while the others slept in. She gave me a nudge with her elbow. "Hey, are you still alive?"

"What time is it?" I muttered.

"A little after six. Do you want coffee?"

"Sure."

Making two cups, she placed mine in front of me, then sat in the chair opposite. "What are you working on?"

I pushed a piece of paper across the table. Dolores picked it up. "This looks complex."

There were three lists on the paper. Each had multiple items. I had spent most of the night trying to fit a square peg into a round hole.

Stone was missing.

Grace Holland was missing. The main suspect there was her former husband. But I couldn't ask him because he was dead. Off to the side, I had the ice issue.

By the time I'd fallen asleep, everything was still a jumble.

I tried to find a link between Grace Holland and Matt Stone. That link was the Kendricks. She was a thorn in their side, and when Stone was investigating, he became one too. Maybe Tyrone decided he needed to be gone and had him disappear.

"Have you found anything out about the detective, Mark?" Dolores asked me.

I shook my head. "Not since he supposedly left town. He was calling at the motel to see if Grace Holland had returned, and then planned to leave from there."

"What's with the drugs?"

"Just a side thing that Larry was working on. It got me interested."

"So what are you trying to do exactly?" Dolores asked.

"Find a link between Grace Holland and Matt Stone."

"That's easy," Dolores said. "The motel."

I frowned at her. "What?"

"Grace Holland was staying at the motel, and Matt Stone went there before he left town. It has to be the motel."

Suddenly, it hit me like a slap in the face. She was right. I'd been too tired the night before to put it together. "Dolores, you are a bloody marvel."

"I am?"

"Yes." I smiled at her. "When I went to the motel the first time to see her, there was a man there that I'd never seen before. He was talking to Jarred Fletcher. When he saw me, he left."

"So?"

"When I asked about the ice coming into town, I was told it was around two months ago, the same time the new owners of the motel arrived."

"Okay, but what does that have to do with the disappearances?"

"What if I'm looking at this wrong? Blaming the wrong person. Looking for something that isn't there."

"Shouldn't you be talking about this with Nicole?"

"Talking to me about what?" Nicole asked in a tired voice as she came into the kitchen. She looked at the mess on the table. "Have you been doing this all night?"

"No, I went to sleep."

"So…tell me what?"

I repeated what I'd just told Dolores.

"So how should you be looking at it?"

"If it hadn't been for Dolores, I wouldn't have put it together. The motel is the key."

"Okay."

"It's not Tyrone Kendrick I should be looking at. It is Jarred and Alice Fletcher."

"The motel owners? Have you been drinking? They're quiet, respectable. No trouble, and—"

"And selling drugs," I said, cutting her off. "Think about it. The ice started coming in the same time they arrived. Grace was staying at the motel, and she was attracting attention from me, but mostly from the police. When I was checking her room, I found some flakes of chipboard from the bedside cupboard on the floor. Alice Fletcher has a sticking plaster on her forehead. Maybe Grace found something out. I don't know."

Nicole nodded. "Okay, genius. What about Matt Stone?"

"Matt Stone went to the motel before he disappeared," I said. "Maybe it was one time too many."

"It's a long stretch," Nicole said.

"But it makes sense," I replied.

Nicole thought for a long time before she let out a sigh. "If you're wrong, Mark, I'll—"

"I'm not. I can feel it."

Nicole picked up the phone. "Suzie, get Byron and meet me at the motel. We're going to search it. I'll just get a warrant."

Thirty minutes later, the warrant was through, and we were all at the motel. Nicole said, "Wait here, Mark. I don't want anything to stuff this up. It was like pulling teeth to get this warrant."

"I won't move."

The detectives were still in town and had taken over once they got wind of it. They went through the motel with a fine-tooth comb. They found where the flakes of chipboard came from and took samples. But it wasn't until they tore apart one of the rooms that was closed for renovations that they found what they were looking for—ice and lots of it.

Both the Fletchers were led to the police vehicles in handcuffs.

———

Four hours of questioning later, Nicole found me asleep behind her desk in her chair. "Mark?"

I rubbed my eyes. "Yeah?"

"Alice just confessed. Told us everything."

I sat up straight. "Grace?"

She nodded.

"Stone?"

"Yes," Nicole confirmed. "Alice was trying to get Grace to leave, but she wouldn't go. They were worried about all the police being around and how it would affect their operation. There was a scuffle, and Grace fell and hit her head. That's what killed her. In the scuffle, Alice sustained an injury that required the plaster on her forehead."

"Christ. What about Stone?"

"He went back and checked over the room. He found the chips on the floor. While he was looking, Jarred panicked and hit him with the hammer he had in his hand. Killed him there. They used bleach to clean the blood up, but there were some parts they missed."

"What happened to the bodies?" I asked.

"They buried them in the riverbed, hoping that the next flow would carry them away."

"Did they give up their supplier?" I asked.

"Yes."

I slumped back in the chair. It was finally over. But for Emily Kendrick, it was only just beginning.

———

That night, there was a knock at the door. When I opened it, I found Eddie Jones, complete with bruises. I'd almost forgotten about him with everything going on. "Eddie, come in."

He shook his head. "I won't stay, Mark. I just wanted to say thank you for what you've done. And I'm sorry that you got into so much trouble."

I smiled, trying to make light of the situation. "One of the hazards of the job, I'm afraid. I'm glad you got what you were looking for."

Eddie reached into his pocket and took out a check. I took it and saw the number. "This is too much, Eddie."

"It's worth it to me."

Putting it in my pocket, I held out my hand, which he took. We shook, and I said, "Take care, Eddie."

"Thanks, Mark."

He turned away, and I watched him leave. Then, I closed the door on that violent chapter of my life.

CHAPTER FIFTY-EIGHT

Two days later, Nicole, Dolores, and I dropped Linda back in Dubbo to catch the plane to Sydney.

"Please stay out of trouble, Mark," she said to me.

"I'll try, but I can't promise anything."

Linda kissed both Nicole and Dolores on the cheek. To her daughter, she said, "Come and visit sometime, huh?"

"Yes, Mum."

"And you," she said to Nicole. "Take care of yourself and that baby girl."

"Always."

We watched her climb onto the plane bus and waved her off. Nicole came over to me and said, "Ready for home?"

"One more place to go," I said.

She knew what I meant. "In that case, Dolores and I will go baby shopping."

Dolores's eyes opened wide. "We will?"

"Yes."

"I hate shopping."

"Good. Come on."

Twenty minutes later, I was in the hospital. I found

Larry sitting up in bed, wide awake. He saw me enter and smiled. "Damn it, Mark. I missed all the action."

"You class getting shot is missing the action?" I asked.

Larry's expression changed. "You found the girl's mother too."

"Yeah. If it hadn't been for you telling me about the ice, I might never have found out."

"I can't believe it was Jarred and Alice."

"Yeah, hiding in plain sight."

"Do you have time to stay a while, Mark?"

I nodded. "Sure."

"Good. Sit down and tell me all about it."

So I did.

A LOOK AT: GENOCIDE (THE GODS OF WAR 1)

Kane and Jensen are hauled before an intelligence committee bent on finding out the truth no matter the consequences...

They are called The Gods of War: Russian Generals who were given birth in the old days of the USSR. They live in the shadows. No one knows their faces. Over the years they have evolved into one of the most dangerous entities in the covert world.

Until they cross the wrong people...

"John 'Reaper' Kane and Raymond 'Knocker' Jensen have been pulled into a new clandestine mission by MI6 to investigate a mysterious gas attack in a Northern Syrian village. As they delve deeper, they unravel a complex conspiracy beyond their wildest expectations. The gas attack is just the tip of a bigger iceberg. And before the two are done, death and destruction will follow them across the globe in their relentless pursuit to expose the truth behind the ominous plans of The Gods of War.

AVAILABLE NOW

ABOUT THE AUTHOR

A relative newcomer to the world of writing, Brent Towns self-published his first book in 2015. *Last Stand in Sanctuary* took him two years to write. His first hardcover book, a Black Horse Western, was published the following year.

Since then, he has written twenty-six western stories, including some in collaboration with British western author, Ben Bridges; several action adventure novels, such as his bestselling *Team Reaper* series; the novelization to the 2019 movie, *Bill Tilghman and the Outlaws*; as well as scripted a handful of Commando Comics. Not bad for an Australian author, he thinks.

Often up until the small hours of the night, bashing away at his tortured keyboard in Queensland, Australia, Brent loves to lose himself in the world of fiction. If you're interested in sharing your thoughts in more detail, scan the QR code below! Your feedback is invaluable to him—and often helps shape his future writing endeavors.